Shots ripped from thickets of low barberry and currant bush. Scared wild, the sorrell swapped ends and took over from there. It smashed off through the brush and broke out onto the meadow. Bishop bent low in the saddle and let the horse use its own best judgment. The gunfire in the brush rapidly gathered volume. The open meadow was slightly safer, perhaps, at that.

He heard the solid tattoo of running horses behind him, and he hipped around, gun in hand to cut down any ambitious tramp who thought to clip him in the back.

L. L. FOREMAN has also written
the following Ace books:

JEMEZ BRAND
LAST STAND MESA
THE PLUNDERING GUN
ROGUES LEGACY
THE SILVER FLAME
POWDERSMOKE PARTNERS

The
Mustang
Trail

L. L. FOREMAN

ace books
A Division of Charter Communications Inc.
1120 Avenue of the Americas
New York, N.Y. 10036

THE MUSTANG TRAIL

Copyright ©, 1965, by L. L. Foreman

An Ace Book, by arrangement with Doubleday & Co., Inc.

All Rights Reserved

I

F<small>ORT</small> G<small>RIFFIN</small> stood on a hill overlooking the town that only officially bore the same name. It had been built and garrisoned as a restraining measure against reservation-shunning Indians who objected to the wholesale slaughter of the buffalo herds. The Indians were inclined to believe that the buffalo was more or less their property, thoughtfully provided by the Great Wakan for their food, raiment, and tepee shelter. White men didn't hold with any such heathen nonsense, and soon a shantytown sprang up as headquarters for the hunters engaged in profitably exterminating the so-called Southern Herd. Someone named it Hell's Half Acre. The name stuck.

The fort now served to guard the West Fork Trail, the cattle trail that ran up the Texas Panhandle and on through the Cherokee Strip to the Kansas railhead. The town had grown to sprawl over considerably more than half an acre, besides gaining in ill fame. It had become a hell-hole since the wipe-out of the buffalo.

Out-of-work hunters lingered on, broke, out to murder any man for a dollar. Wild trail hands stopped over for a fast whirl and got it. Cattlemen fought each other for grab-rights to the buffalo-cleared range. Soldiers from the fort swaggered on the prod. Freighters and mule-skinners made a knuckly crowd.

And always a dangerous sprinkling of badmen, outlaws, thieves, and killers from everywhere. They had to drift, staying a jump ahead of tracks scored on dark back trails, congregating vagrantly wherever the law, if any, was loose and spread thin. No man owning anything worth stealing went unarmed in Hell's Half Acre, or walked alone in the dark.

To cap it, Fort Griffin was now buying horses, all it could get, top price. For the Army.

There had been the bloody battles of Powder River and the Rosebud, followed by the stunning disaster on the Little Big Horn. General Custer of the 7th Cavalry—George Armstrong Custer, dashing young hero of the Civil War, impetuous and headstrong Indian fighter, the undefeatable Long Hair—was gone to glory with nigh three hundred of his troopers. The victorious Sioux and Cheyenne were rampaging on the warpath.

Remounts urgently needed for the newly increased Army, came the call. Bring on your mustangs. If they're anywhere near fit for cavalrymen to ride against the hostiles, bring them on. Fort Griffin and other Army posts of the West were buying horses to remount the broken and vengeful 7th, the 5th; the Army waited impatiently to take to the field on combat campaign.

THE MUSTANG TRAIL

Here was a rich new source of revenue, made to order for broke and desperate men. Who's got a horse that meets Army requirements? The Army demands a clear title, a bill of sale, before buying.

Okay, soldier—can do. Plenty of people around able to use a clever and convincing pen. First get the horse. Kill the owner. Go through his pockets for extras.

In less than half a year the West Fork Trail had become known as the Mustang Trail, haunted by horse thieves who could tell at a glance if a rider's horse would meet the Army's basic requirements: sixteen hands high, solid color preferred, passably good build and sound wind, gentled so it at least wouldn't wipe the moon at the flap of a saddle blanket.

A new prosperity trickled into Hell's Half Acre, to lodge sooner or later in the town's dives and deadfalls. It drew a fresh influx of gamblers and Lulu girls from other parts.

A four-horse wagon came banging down the crooked street, wheels slewing in and out of dry ruts and scooping up dust. It carried a solid load of some sort, canvas-covered, securely roped down.

So did its driver carry a load, but less securely. He was crazy drunk, roaring through town and using all the street, not caring if he crushed man or woman, stirring up a stamping flurry among horses tied to the hitchrails. His filthy rags of buckskins showed him to be a buffalo tramp—most likely one of the brush thugs who, without trade, rarely recognized by any of the regular skinning crews, called themselves buffalo hunters. His matted mane of coarse black hair proclaimed some Indian blood, possibly Tonkawa. Drink always thickened the heavy features of the Tonk strain.

A bevy of Lulu girls, crossing from the Shackelford House to the Bee Hive, scattered out of the way, emitting screams and forceful comments. There were no ladies in Hell's Half Acre.

Emerging from the Brazos Hotel, and also bound for the Bee Hive, Mr. Rogate Bishop glanced up from clipping the end of a fresh cigar with a razor-sharp clasp knife. The wagon rushed at him. He saw the driver grinning like a madman.

Casually agile, Mr. Rogate Bishop jumped back, but not before stroking the knife in a reaching sweep and slicing the near lines clean through. He also jabbed the driver's whip-arm. Then, lighting his cigar, he calmly watched to see what would happen.

What happened was plenty, for the rambunctious driver. Being drunk and belligerent, he tried to haul in for a fight over the matter. His lines swerved the half-wild, racing team. His wagon sideswiped Murphy's Bar, crashed into the Star Hall at the bend, and he kited off headlong among the floundering horses. By the time he scrambled clear of the tangle, Murphy and the Star Hall proprietor were out demanding payment for damages—each with a sawed-off shotgun cocked for argument.

"That was neat!" one of the Lulus called to Bishop, and the others bestowed looks of warm approval and favor upon him.

But his mind was on poker. He touched the wide brim of his black hat to them and went on over into the Bee Hive. There, soon deep in the constructive enterprise of matching cards into profitable sequences, he forgot the matter.

It was only an incident. Should repercussions happen to follow, he would handle them as they came along. In a place like Hell's Half Acre it wasn't possible to avoid occasional trouble and still enjoy life, liberty, and the pursuit of fortune. Something was forever cropping up. All you had to do was stay alert day and night.

"One," Bishop murmured, dealing. He drew to three jacks and an ace, and filled, not to his surprise.

This round, he mused, something more than a winning hand might be needed to rake in the pot. Probably a gun. The rusty-haired young Texan across the table, for one, was growing restless, running out of chips. And, come a challenge, Rusty would have help on his side. Besides the three other dissatisfied losers in the game, there were quite a few hardcases in the Bee Hive who seriously resented Bishop's unbroken run of luck since his arrival some days back. And there were Texans present, too.

Well, that was the way it generally ran. To expect profit with safety was asking too much. He had packed his winnings out of other tough towns, one way or another.

"Raise ten," said Bishop when the pot was healthy.

The red-haired Texan counted his remaining chips and shoved them in. "Call."

Bishop spread his cards face up and leaned back. The other players, two boss freighters and an ambitious tinhorn, had dropped out. The Texan scraped his chair and stood up, reading Bishop's full house, three jacks and ace pair. He was young and tough, too shabbily dressed to be bucking a no-limit game.

He said, "Where I grew up they shoot men for that!"

Bishop returned moderately, "Where you grew up they should teach the younguns not to bet into a one-card draw, unless they think the man's bluffing." And then he, too, came to his feet.

He was tall and looked severe. His black coat hung open, allowing sight of two belts studded with rows of brass cartridges. That was for well-meant warning. His black hat, fingered down on the right side of the broad brim, lent a rakish hint to his austere air. He had a muscled face, strong and dark, from which a pair of slate-gray eyes glimmered cold query.

While he pinned his gaze waitingly on the Texan, giving him his choice, he missed little of what went on in the crowded barroom. Keeping check was a habit of his senses, routine. A man could never afford to let down, if he was a loner in this kind of life, and he had embarked on it long ago and made enemies in many strange quarters.

Not quite mad enough to push the issue to its exploding point, the Texan jerked his lean shoulders and paced off. The game broke up. Hungrily watched by hostile eyes, Bishop gathered up his stacks of chips and cashed them in.

He was drinking at the bar, deciding on his manner of exit from the Bee Hive, when the Texan ranged up along-side and admitted, "I didn't actually spot any monkey-shines there in your game. Nobody else did, either, I guess. It went too fast to catch."

"Luck's a fast lady," observed Bishop. "Changeable. She comes through all right, though, with a little encourage-ment."

The Texan inclined his head in polite agreement. "My name's Delaney. Friends call me Red."

"I wonder why." Privately, Bishop also wondered why the redhead was tendering him a friendly opening. "Bishop, me. Rogate Bishop. Friends," he added drily, "call me Mr. Bishop."

Red Delaney made a wry mouth. "Friends?" He turned away, and swung back again, sighing. "A town full of poker tables—and I go bucking 'Rogue' Bishop's game! What did I do to deserve that, on top of other misfortunes?"

10

THE MUSTANG TRAIL

"You only dropped four hundred dollars," Bishop said, letting the use of his nickname pass, though he didn't care for it. He hadn't chosen that nickname; it had become attached to him. "If your loss hurts so bad, I'll loan some back to you, just to keep my shoulder dry."

"Mr. Bishop, those words are hard for me to swallow!"

"Wash 'em down with a drink."

"Thanks. You pay for it. I can't, as of now."

Bishop rapped on the bar. "A drink for Mr. Delaney, and another for me." He wasn't getting onto a first-name or nickname stage of fellowship with a busted cowpuncher.

"On a silver tray?" asked the bartender, heavily sarcastic. Then catching Bishop's level stare at him, he said respectfully, "Coming right up!"

They drank together. Red Delaney set his emptied glass on the bar, and said, "I've got a paying proposition for a man with some ready money. A kind of business investment."

Bishop nodded. "Hum!" These damned Texans. Insulted by an offer of cash, but ready to rook you out of it. That accounted for the friendly opening.

"I'm flat broke," Red Delaney confided, which to Bishop was needless information and uninteresting to boot. "I started out from way down in Refugio with horses to sell to the Army. Second night out, a gang of thieves stampeded the bunch and got every last one of 'em. I came on up here to watch for 'em. Fort Griffin's the likeliest place where they'll show up, by far. I had some money. Spent part. You cleaned up the rest of it."

"Offhand, I'd say you're unlucky."

"Seems like it, for a fact, this trip. But on the other hand I made mistakes, like playing poker with a shark. I don't put much stock in luck, tell you the truth."

Neither did Bishop. Not trustingly. Nerve and highly

11

trained hands, plus a disregard for risky consequences, were a lot more reliable. More faithfully productive of results. He had scuffed deep tracks, carelessly scored up a notorious reputation, yet stayed always himself—a remote kind of man, cool, with a dry sense of humor that verged on the sardonic; essentially a loner who bet straight on his own ability to boot fortune into line with his own desires.

Shifting the subject, Red Delaney said, "You ever hear of the big die-up a few years ago, down the trail? A freak blizzard caught three or four trail herds, and they bunched in a kind of hollow. All the cattle froze there. Their bones nigh fill that hollow. It's called the Boneyard, in fact."

"I've seen it. And," Bishop said, "I've smelled it!"

"So've I. Here's the deal. You put up the money for wagons and teams, and for hiring a crew. I'll take the job of hauling the bones up to the railroad."

"What the hell for?"

"To ship north," Red Delaney explained. "They grind 'em up for fertilizer. There's money in it. We'll split fifty-fifty on the profit. How about it?"

Bishop's headshake was positive. "A smelly deal if I ever heard one!" He rapped on the bar for more drinks. "Bone-picking! That's getting down pretty low!"

Red Delaney flushed. "Not saying I like it. I need a stake bad to get me started again, is all. Those horses of mine, I guess they're gone for good by now. Damn thieves must've taken 'em some other place. All right, I've got another proposition."

"Save it!"

"You can listen, can't you? Not far from the Boneyard, there's a place called the Sandhole, over by the Guadalupe River. It's a low patch of fine sand, hard-packed. You can walk or ride on it. But when the river rises and seeps into it, then the Sandhole's a quicksand. Still looks solid, but you'd sink right in. A big rock sticks up on the far side from the trail. Years ago some Indians used it for a trap."

Bishop swallowed his drink and motioned for the bartender to make free again with the bottle. "What kind of trap?" The subject didn't come near to touching his interest, but he had won money off this would-be bone-picker, after all, and guessed perhaps he owed him some slight consideration.

"A man trap," Red Delaney said. "For white men. See, it was just a little bunch of Indians—they were said to be a Pima family that wandered away from their tribe, or got thrown out and went renegade on the quiet. One of 'em, a girl, would stand up on top of that rock, not a stitch of clothes on, and entice a passing traveler to—uh—investigate. Some of those Pima girls are downright beautiful. I guess she was, all right."

"Quit licking your lips!" Bishop grunted. He, too, had seen some luscious Pima girls.

Red Delaney coughed. "Well, a quicksand, you know how it is. The man would ride right into it, looking up at that girl. Before he could struggle out of it, the Pimas would slip an arrow in him and let him sink. They took his horse and saddle, which was what they were after. Got several that way, till the river went down and the Sandhole turned dry again. The girl was s'posed to be a *chisera*—a witch— and the rock's been called Crazy Chisera Rock ever since."

"She wasn't so crazy," remarked Bishop. "But you are, if you've got any idea you're pretty enough to stand up naked on a rock like a siren enticing the weary wayfarer to—"

"Whoa!" Red Delaney protested. "Listen. An uncle of mine got caught there. He was coming home from selling a beef herd, loaded with cash. Far as I could ever find out, the *chisera* waved to him, and he—"

"Old goat!"

"Well, maybe he thought she needed help," Red argued, with faint conviction. "He was a gentleman, my Uncle Wesley, and a deacon of the church. Always ready with a helping hand. Anyhow, he sank in the quicksand, all his money on him. That was years ago. The Sandhole's dry as a bone now. I don't know how deep it goes, nor how far down a body sinks when it's a quicksand. We can hire the digging done for—"

"We what?" Bishop interrupted. "Why, you sacrilegious son! First it's bone-picking, now it's body-snatching!"

Red worked his jaw for a moment, chewing down a cud of temper. He said, after taking a drink, "Look, I'd see to it my Uncle Wesley got Christian burial, and any other bodies we found in there. The money we'd split between us. I don't see anything much wrong about that."

"My eyesight's too good," murmured Bishop. He hadn't any itch to invest his money in a grave, wet or dry. "Digging up corpses? No, grave-robbing's out of my line! Let your old goat of an uncle rest there along with the others."

Swallowing again, Red remarked, "I'm surprised you're more fussy than me, considering who you are and some of the things I've heard about you!"

Bishop rolled a broad shoulder. "I draw the line at ghouls."

"You do, eh?" said Red Delaney in the softest of Texas drawls. "Well, I draw the line at you calling me that!" He lashed a terrific punch for Bishop's jaw.

Cat-quick, Bishop fended it off with his left forearm, followed through with a driving thrust, and set himself to business. He wasted no motions.

Shoved back onto his worn-over high heels, Red Delaney for that instant balanced wide open to receive what was coming. He got it—Bishop's right fist, wickedly accurate, square between the eyes. He hurtled rearward, spilling men and drinks for half the length of the bar. While he lay goggling, the Bee Hive buzzed into action.

II

SETTING OFF a riot in Hell's Half Acre never called for
much special effort, day or night, and here in the crowded
Bee Hive were sharp-edged men with tempers easily jarred.
Texas trail hands and soldiers nursed a mutual antipathy.
Freighters and teamsters, thundering lords of the road, were
touchy when caught afoot. Buffalo tramps and Tonk half-
breeds, despised for their debauched poverty, were always
ready to slip a knife into anybody better than themselves.
And the tinhorn coterie shared a common grudge against
Bishop.

Beginning with the upset customers along the bar, a brisk
fight broke out, Bishop its main focal point, Red Delaney un-
derfoot. It spread like wildfire into a free-for-all, every
scrapper pitching in to knock off a score on somebody and
the screeching Lulus darting to exits.

Bishop got his back to the bar and struck out at all who
charged within his reach, on the sound theory that he had
no friends here and therefore didn't need to use discrimina-
tion. It hadn't been any part of his intention to set off a
riot in the place, but such spontaneous eruptions were too
common to disconcert him, and he figured before the uproar ended he could be out of the Bee Hive with his winnings. In a sardonic fashion he appreciated the mad humor
of it, until a tinhorn cheaply flung an empty bottle that
barely missed nailing him on the ear.

17

"Hum?" he growled, dodging another. "Bottles?" He had a plentiful supply of bottles behind him. Full ones, at that.

Booting a bellowing mule-skinner out of his way to make space, he vaulted over the bar. He helped himself from the tier of backbar shelves, and—while the bartender howled anguish for his precious stock—sent bottles flying to where they could do the most good. The crash of each bottle punctuated the uproar, and doors began flapping, tamer souls seeking the sunny street along with the Lulus. He could keep this up while the stock lasted.

A big-hatted cattleman dug out a Dragoon .44 and cocked it in Bishop's direction. Bishop took him up on that, fast, before the affair grew too seriously lethal. He brushed back his coat and a blue gunbarrel dully gleamed. It spurted brightly, and the big hat flipped. The cattleman thought first to grab for his hat. A second bullet cut the brim, and he let it go skimming and put away his Dragoon .44, knowing a gunfighter when he saw one.

The doors banged busily. Encouraging the exodus, Bishop tipped a shot at the pool table. The cue ball went wild and englished all over the green baize. When it hobbled to rest, badly chipped, the Bee Hive was occupied mainly by some Texans too proud to run, and a few unconditioned unfortunates on the floor, Red Delaney among them.

An Army major appeared from somewhere in the lengthening hush. He straightened his hat, tugged wrinkles from his coat, and stared sternly around. "No more of that, now!" he snapped, marching out. Nobody paid him notice.

"Gentlemen," Bishop asked the Texans, "what'll you have?" He holstered his gun, letting them see that he wore a mate to it, for insurance in emergency. "I'm in a position to offer anything you name as long as it's whisky."

They grinned, relaxing. "Make it whisky!"

The bartender took over the job of serving from the re-

mains of his stock. The Texans solemnly rebuked him for keeping a messy establishment, glass littering the whisky-puddled
floor, windows and mirrors cracked, the pool table not fit
to play on. Bishop inquired the amount of his bill. The
bartender did some rapid accounting in his head and arrived at a round figure.

"Fifteen hundred dollars ought to about square it."

"Okay, thief." Bishop paid, thinning his money belt. "Somebody hoist Mr. Delaney up to the bar so he can join us
in the next round."

A Texan stuck his thumb at a front window. "Want to
buy that Yankee sojer-boss a drink?" he queried ironically.
"He's waitin' out theah."

Bishop nodded. "I noticed. Let him buy his own."

The major had halted outside. He did appear to be
waiting for somebody to come out of the Bee Hive. He
fidgeted, throwing impatient looks at the doors.

Bishop saw no possible connection between the major's
waiting and the recent brawl. The officers of the fort held
no authority over Hell's Half Acre and the doings of its
residents. He hadn't any reason to believe that he was the
awaited one, either, until the major came close to the window, caught his eye, and beckoned to him.

That struck him as odd. Cavalry officers had their faults
and peculiarities, some of them. Overseverity, laxness, hard
drinking, heavy gambling. And bullheaded bravery. Like
Captain Fetterman storming up Massacre Hill against orders,
to die with eighty men in a bloody ambush. Like Custer
at the Little Big Horn, disregarding the warnings of his
Indian scouts, charging off into disaster.

But furtiveness? Well, no. Yet this major was being furtive. It deserved looking into. Bishop had one more drink
with the Texans, and left.

19

"I am Major Jennisk." The major had a thin, snapping voice, and after speaking he pressed his lips together as if he had thundered a proclamation.

"My name's Bishop."

"Yes." Major Jennisk didn't offer his hand, nor give a nod. "I was impressed in there by how you handled that mixed mob. Most impressed. Let's walk up the hill. I have a proposition to put to you."

"Bones?" Bishop inquired. Enterprising propositioners seemed to crop up frequently around here.

"What? No, of course not!"

"Bodies?"

The major showed some confusion. "What are you talking about?" He had trouble matching his pace to Bishop's long-legged stride. "Bones and bodies—I hope you're not drunk!"

Bishop lighted a cigar and said nothing. At a glance he checked off Jennisk as a desk soldier. This soft-skinned man, with his pursed mouth and piping voice, couldn't be imagined as a field officer leading hard-bitten cavalry, guidons proudly whipping, sabers aloft in a charge, bugle blaring. His polished boots were unmarked by any wear of stirrups. His blues and shoulder straps could not remove from him the look of a somewhat paunchy and untanned businessman.

No mistaking his kind. The Army of the West had a share of them and they tended to run to type. Commissions won on the political field by string-pulling: administrative jobs, and promotions won for tenure and paperwork—while the rank and file fought to keep the trails open, trooped half-dead back to the post, and rode doggedly out again with cleaned carbines loose in saddleboots.

When out of Hell's Half Acre and walking up the hill toward the fort, Major Jennisk spoke again. "A man of your kind, Bishop—"

"My kind?" Bishop picked him up curtly.

"Your caliber, I mean. You're wasting yourself. Wasting your talents on gambling and fighting."

"A poker game once in a while ends up in a fight," Bishop conceded. "It's a common disease of bad losers. I don't push for it. I get enough of that in my other trade—troubleshooting." His troubleshooting had covered a wide and varied range of activities, usually violent and often widely outside of the law, but that was what he chose to call it.

"There are better things," Jennisk observed.

Bishop removed his cigar to spit out a flake of tobacco. "Such as?"

"Such as helping to obtain badly needed remounts for the gallant soldiers of our army!" Jennisk responded. "A most worthy and patriotic occupation. And—ah—profitable," he added less piously. "My orders are to buy up to a thousand head as soon as possible. Remounts for Generals Crook, Mackenzie, and Miles. Of course, the horses must come reasonably close to meeting Army requirements, you understand."

"Yeah."

"So far, I haven't been able to fill half the order. I'm in receipt of—ah—pressing communications in reference to the subject. The people at divisional headquarters don't realize my difficulties," Jennisk complained. "They think a procurement officer, here in the West, only has to snap his fingers to get hold of a thousand horses overnight!"

"It's horse country, they know that much."

"Yes, but these cow ponies are mostly undersize. The Army isn't taking broomtail broncs."

Bishop kept silent, inwardly speculating as to where this was leading. Something was in the wind, involving him.

Jennisk frowned irritably at having to carry the bulk of conversation. Reticence was a military perquisite, to be used

THE MUSTANG TRAIL

in bolstering a stiff and unapproachable dignity. Mere civilians
hadn't the right to be laconic toward an officer. It smacked of
disrespect.

In a moment he said, "A man came to me some days ago,
a Mexican. He said he had a crew camped down the trail
with three hundred good, big horses. He had come on up
here to look into the selling prospects. From the way he
went about it, asking questions and not saying much, I
judged he couldn't show title to the horses. Stole them
somewhere, I'll be bound. Otherwise he'd have brought them
straight on up to the fort, eh?"

"Sounds like it."

"Yes. However, in the light of the Army's urgent need
of good horses, I—hem—decided to stretch a point." Jennisk
paused. His sharp round eyes swept sidelong over Bishop's
impassive face. He cleared his throat and said, "I offered
him twenty-five dollars a head."

"What's the buying price now for Army remounts?" Bishop
inquired. He knew the answer. His speculations were reaching toward conclusions.

"One hundred and twenty-five."

Bishop did some rapid mental figuring. He quirked a dark
eyebrow at the result "Hum! Three hundred horses, that
price, cost the Army thirty-seven thousand and five hundred dollars, right? But at your offer to him of twenty-five
a head, it comes to seven thousand five hundred. Who'd
get the thirty-thousand-dollars difference? You? Man, there
are better things than poker! Graft, for one!"

Something distasteful puckered Jennisk's small mouth. "I
call it business! The Army would get its horses, paying no
more than the regular price. That Mexican would have done
well to take seven thousand five hundred for his stolen
horses. He'll never get more anywhere else, without showing
title to them." His eyes narrowed. "Damned scoundrel in-

22

sulted me and walked out! He'll be sorry he didn't do business with me!"

"Meaning you can send out word on him?" Bishop suggested. "Block his other possible markets?" He felt some slight sympathy for that Mexican horse thief. Tough enough, lifting horses, without running afoul of a gouging grafter.

"I could, but I won't." Jennisk brought his eyes around again to Bishop's face. He stated with slow emphasis, "My offer is still open! Twenty-five dollars a head for those three hundred horses, no title asked. Paperwork goes over my desk, so I'll take care of that. And I don't care who delivers them! Well?"

Bishop shook his head. "Not enough. I'd have to pick and hire a a fighting crew—"

"No, you wouldn't," Jennisk broke in. "Your crew is already picked and hired. At my expense. They're captained by a one-time buffalo hunter who calls himself Hump. They're camped near a place known as the Sandhole, along the Guadalupe. Hump is a very tough dog, but he's half crazy like most of his breed. I can't rely on him to stay sober and get the job done. But I'll have to, unless you go down there and take charge. It calls for somebody like you, a man who can handle a rough gang." He gnawed his upper lip, and said reluctantly, "Thirty dollars a head, delivered. That's a clear profit to you of nine thousand dollars."

"And twenty-eight thousand five hundred to you!"

"Army retirement pay isn't much. A man must look to his future. Must make the most of his opportunities."

Bishop reconsidered. Raiding a horse-thief camp didn't clash with his broadminded principles. Stolen horses were open game. And besides, his money belt was light since paying for the Bee Hive damage.

"Forty," he said. "I've got to take along some jigger who knows the country down there and can trail-boss a band of

23

horses that size. And willing to do any fool thing for money. Got the right boy in mind, but he's a damned Texan and I'll have to offer him a fair cut."

"Thirty-five, then, blast it!"

"Major, you've good as bought three hundred good, big horses for the gallant soldiers of the Army of the West— a worthy and patriotic occupation! *Hasta la vista!*"

"All right, until I see you—"

"That's what I said. You ought to pick up a little Span- ish before you retire from your rugged campaigning, sol- dier. It might've helped you get along better with that Mexican horse thief. Your tough dog calls himself Hump, you said?"

"Hump, yes. I'll give you a note to him. Watch he doesn't get drunk and let you down."

"I'll try to keep him humping."

III

Riding down the last stretch of Plum Creek to the Guadalupe River, Red Delaney remarked to Bishop that they would be getting to the Sandhole pretty soon.

Red said it with a wistful note to his voice. He had not given up his idea of excavating Uncle Wesley and various other defunct gentlemen who had fallen prey to the fetching *chisera* and her Pima family, and giving them all decent Christian burial. With profit.

But the Sandhole held nothing for Bishop. Its corpsed victims of romantic fervor could forever lie undisturbed, as far as he was concerned. Their cash value was speculative, probably nil. He dealt as a rule in ventures more positive of results and less laborsome, such as drawing to three jacks and an ace, himself dealing.

Still, the Sandhole meant meeting up soon with the Hump gang, and scouting the camp of the Mexican horse thieves. Bishop allowed himself to become interested in it to that extent, meantime deploring his dwindling stock of cigars, the loss of a full quart of whisky that had got broken, and the scarcity of good food.

Along here the trail grooved like an immensely wide and shallow ditch past clumps of forest, a brown scar carved by northbound Texas herds. Skulls and ribbed skeletons of cows, toothed bare by coyotes, marked the route. At day's travel spaces lay the great bare patches of the bedding grounds, with their broken monuments of wornout and abandoned wagons—stripped of ironware by roving Indians—where Texas trail outfits had camped for the night.

"Plain digging," Red said, deep in his thoughts of resurrection. "That's all it'd take. Uncle Wesley, I bet, was loaded down with maybe twenty thousand dollars."

"To hell with your uncle!" growled Bishop. "He most likely spent his money on Lulus before he started home to his wife!"

Three days in the saddle, plain grub and nothing to drink but water, and he was souring on this affair. He was cogitating ways to sweeten it. Jennisk would go to forty dollars a head for the horses, if pushed hard. Or fifty. Sixty? Jennisk had to fill his order, and was hungry for graft. Seventy or eighty? Hell, no man had to feel bound by any agreement with that shifty toad.

Red grinned, and said, "Uncle Wesley never got married, and he wasn't too loose with a dollar. I'll know what to do with my cut of your horse money, if we get it. Maybe first I'll look further into the Boneyard prospects. That's it ahead."

Bishop blew through his nose. "I smell it. You and your bones!"

Without doubt an unpleasant odor did hang in the air, and Red nodded, saying that the stink was the part that just might discourage him from taking up bone-selling. "The Sandhole's over that way, nearer the river. This Hump feller and his crew—they're not expecting us, huh?"

"No. Jennisk said we'd find 'em somewhere around there, this side of the Mexican camp—wherever that is, and if it's still there." Bishop touched up his horse. "Let's get out of this perfume."

"Strangers ahead!" Red warned presently—and unnecessarily, Bishop having already noted and sized up the group of riders coming out at them from the cottonwoods along the river.

A down-at-heel crew, this. They wore blackened tatters of buckskins and rode rib-raw Indian ponies. Buffalo tramps, all, frowzy and unwashed, most of them wearing dirty head-rags to hold back their shoulder-length hair. But every one of them carried a shining new Henry repeater rifle slung across the saddle.

"Phew!" Red breathed. "What hell's backdoor let out that pack?"

Bishop said, a cold detachedness in his voice, "Hump's crew, I guess." And then, saturninely, "If the big duck in front is Hump himself, the Boneyard's not the only thing that stinks in this game! I croppered him in Hell's Half Acre, and I doubt he's ready to overlook it."

"Your celebrated luck, Mr. Bishop, seems to've slipped!"

"On this particular deal, Mr. Delaney, I didn't shuffle the cards. Jennisk drew this lot, damn him!"

Bishop's tone carried no hint of worry, but his deepset eyes glimmered like tarnished silver wiped across by a reflection of flame. This was a bad break. By their looks the oncoming rabble had been getting in some heavy drinking lately.

They met on the cattle-carved trail, no cover within short reach, and pulled to a stand. It became evident that Hump was by habit more Indian than white man, for he started to raise his right hand in greeting—a transparently faithless gesture, giving him a moment to measure Bishop and Delaney.

A perverse spirit caused Bishop to give him likewise an Indian greeting. "How!" he drawled, and stared at him.

Into Hump's gross face washed a look of recognition, swiftly followed by scowling rage. His rising right hand fell to his Henry repeater, while he wrenched his pony broadside, and by the motion—a drunken maneuver—he made clear his intention.

Bishop rapped harshly, "Wup—snub it!" He brushed back his coat. He watched until the clawing hand stilled, and he drew out the note that Jennisk had written. "This is for you, if you're Hump. And if you can read."

Hump could read, after a fashion, his thick lips working on the words of Jennisk's message. He raised a wildly bitter glare.

"Says here you're the cap'n! Says you're in charge!"

Intolerable resentment gusted a curse from him. His crew of buffalo tramps leaned forward, glowering, catching his fury, without full comprehension of its cause.

"*You!*"

"Right!" said Bishop, and he too leaned forward in his saddle. A startlingly satanic smile creased his dark face. He knew the breed of badman he had to deal with, and was gambling for prompt dominance. Nothing less would do. "Me—Mr. Rogate Bishop! You don't like it?"

"No! No, you—"

"Then we'll iron out your objections, right now!"

Red Delaney held his breath. Hump's gang numbered seventeen, well armed with their new Henry rifles. Seventeen men of mixed races, brush thugs degraded to savagery by shiftless poverty, barbarous practices, drink, and natural bent. And there sat Rogue Bishop, smiling his devil's smile, tossing arrogant challenge at their leader. It was enough to make the imps of chance shudder. It made Red Delaney regret patronizing the Bee Hive.

And yet his crazed glare dimming, Hump sighed heavily like a Navajo harried by indecision, and looked away from Bishop's eyes. His fury banked for the time being, he muttered raggedly, "I don't like it, but if the major says so—"

"Where's the Mexican outfit?" Bishop demanded at once.

Hump pointed downriver with his chin. "This side, 'bout a long rifle-shot b'low Sandhole. They don't know yet we're here."

"They'll know tonight, early."

"What? Not till I git more men. That'n's a border outfit. Tough. Know their business."

"So do I," said Bishop. He outstared the black, blood-shot eyes. "I'm giving the orders, Hump. You've got all the men we need, and I don't figure to hang around here wait-ing for more. First, I want a look at that camp. Push on!"

Riding with Bishop behind the shabby desperadoes, Red exclaimed hushedly, "Man, oh, man! The pick of a thorny crop! And we work with 'em? I'd as lief prance barefoot in a nest of rattlers! Notice the new rifles? Army issue, those."

Bishop nodded, thinking of Hump's wagon careening down the street of Hell's Half Acre. No question about it, its strapped and canvas-covered load had been the new Henrys and ammunition, supplied by Jennisk at government expense.

Hump's venom spread out and infected the minds of his followers. They kept fiddling with those new .44 rifles, and peering back at Bishop and Red—behavior most impolite in Western country. Bishop silently cursed Jennisk. He was build-ing up a definite dislike for that grafting officer.

As for Red, he hitched his holster forward, yanked his hat down, and muttered something about if only Uncle Wes-ley could see him now, the company he was in. They passed the Sandhole—it wasn't a hole at all, it was flat—and the overlooking Crazy Chisera Rock, and drifted carefully in under the cottonwoods along the bank of the river.

The Mexican outfit had picked a good site for a camp. It was a long meadow, clear of trees and brush, running up over a rise at the next bend of the river. Thick brush flanked it on both sides, so the men didn't have to spend much energy on keeping the band of horses from straying.

They appeared to be unhurriedly packing up, preparing to break camp. They were big-hatted, lean men who moved with the languid agility of riders of the border country where heat imposed economy of action. They would hit the trail *mañana*, perhaps *mañana-mañana*. To somewhere. No rush. *Poco tiempo*—you lived longer and enjoyed it.

Bishop watched from the cottonwoods. "Doesn't look like any three hundred horses to me," he commented to Red. "More like two hundred. Damn it, this thing gets worse right along!"

"A hundred horses short, at thirty-five a head—that's thirty-five hundred dollars we're out of pocket already. And the job's only started, no guar'ntee we can pull it off." Red shook his head. "The Sandhole looks better to me. It's a sure—"

"Shut up!"

Red didn't shut up. He said, "When you told me about three hundred stolen horses down here, I thought maybe—just maybe—they might be mine. It was three hundred good horses I got robbed of, and I think it was some Mexicans who took 'em. Well, those horses up yonder ain't mine. They belong to somebody else. Even if we can take 'em, they're not ours to sell."

"No?"

"Not rightly."

Regarding it as a trifling distinction, Bishop said, "We'll straighten that out later!" This redheaded Texan was either getting religion, or else he'd been raised on a set of outlandish principles. Willing to dig up his late lamented uncle for a stake, yet squeamish when it came to cashing in on somebody's stolen horses. He'd have to be taught the error of his ways, possibly with a gun barrel if he proved stubborn.

30

Bishop spoke to Hump. "Take your mob and circle wide around up there to the top of the rise. Time it so you edge in at sundown. The moon won't come up till about an hour later. In that hour, while it's dark, we get those horses!"

"How?"

"You wait for my signal—two shots. You sing out like you're the law, and shoot high, but keep to cover. Those hombres are way off their home range. It's a fair bet they'll scoot, if they think you're big law—Rangers, or a posse of deputies. So don't let 'em see you. The sight of you wouldn't fool 'em worth a damn!"

Hump lifted a corner of his upper lip, hating the blunt remark, hating to take orders from Bishop. "An' what'll you two hotshots be doin' while we carry the load?"

"We'll move on near the bottom of the meadow, and cut loose when you do. Any who head this way, we'll turn 'em back. We don't want 'em giving us trouble later. We want 'em running clear out of the country, thinking it's full of law. *Sabe?*"

"I *sabe* that, yeah. But the horses—who gits to sell the horses, hunh?"

"They're sold—contracted for at Fort Griffin. You know that. If you've got any idea about selling 'em somewhere else, forget it!"

"How much do we git?" Hump persisted.

"That's between you and Major Jennisk," Bishop answered him. "You're on his private payroll. Now get going. Lay off the booze, and don't botch the trick!"

His cool presumption, necessary yet dangerous, lighted a repetition of the wild glare. Hump sucked in a noisy breath. His black-nailed fingers spoked out and stiffly clawed air. Then he whirled around and grunted to his buffalo tramps, and he and they drifted off silently like malevolent ghosts, leading their scrawny ponies.

31

"And after tonight—then what?" Red muttered. "We'll be three days on the trail to Fort Griffin—riding with 'em, camping with 'em. They'll knife us, first chance in the dark!"

"If we give 'em the chance," Bishop agreed. "We'll try not to do that. You getting spooky?"

"Yeah, a little. How about you?"

"A little."

IV

THERE WERE hours to wait before dark. They rode part way back toward the Sandhole, picketed their horses and aired the saddles, and ate dried beef and biscuits. No coffee. A fire was out of the question. They sneaked a smoke, though, squatting tiredly after the trek down from Fort Griffin.

On that trek Red had came to know Bishop's long silences and to respect them, and he didn't speak until the tree shadows stretched purple.

"I swear, Bishop, I don't look forward to camping with that bunch," he admitted. "They stink! Hump's that crazy-mean he's liable to do anything. They're the kind that used to scalp-hunt Yaquis for the Mexican bounty—and took Mexican scalps when they ran short of Yaquis! Women's and kids'. Trimmed 'em to look Yaqui. Ten pesos each."

"I know."

"Don't tell me you did it!"

Bishop looked at him. "You want my fist in your teeth?"

"Sorry—didn't mean that. Guess I'm keyed up."

"Keep your hair on."

"I only hope I can!"

At last Bishop crushed an inch of burning cigar into the earth, and murmured, "Let's go, Red." He spoke the name unconsciously, his mind foraging ahead.

That casual use of his nickname was quietly pleasing to Red Delaney. He knew the kind of company he was in, and it meant something to hear this self-contained man call him Red without thinking of it.

Red responded, rising, "Okay." Then, feeling that this was not enough: "I'm ready, Rogue." He didn't realize the liberty he took, nor Bishop's forbearance in allowing it.

They left their horses and went forward on foot to the spot where Hump had parted from them, and crawled from there to the foot of the sloping meadow. A patch of dwarf willows tempted them on farther, and they eased in and waited.

Voices came down to them, the words indistinguishable, the cadences fluidly Mexican. They heard somebody breaking up deadwood. Those sounds sank to comfortable murmuring around a cookfire torched against the graying light of sundown. Three or four men were leisurely saddling up, chatting back and forth. A peaceful camp of cheerful horse thieves contented with their lot. The western glow faded toward the brief twilight that within twenty minutes would be blackness.

Twenty minutes to go. Red glanced at Bishop, and could read there only what appeared to be calm meditation. Chewing on a fresh cigar, unlighted, Bishop was passing the time in trimming a broken fingernail with his clasp knife.

Red rolled his shoulders restlessly. Horses were his line. He could take care of himself in a rough spot, but trouble was not his trade, as it was Bishop's. The big man simply accepted peril as a normal part of his life, an everyday gambling hazard.

"Couple readying to ride night watch," Red reported, for something to say. "That's not a bad camp. Must be a spring near, or maybe they water the horses down at the river. Good grass. Wonder how they do for . . . What the hootin' hell!"

With the light yet a deepening blue-gray, minutes more

34

to go, Bishop was still engaged in scraping smooth his fingernail when the mischief broke loose. At a yelling outburst, and Red's exclamation, he sprang up—and saw mad
disaster.

It caught him unready. He couldn't blame himself too
much for that. All logical prediction had to be predicated
upon sanity, and the sharpest brain could not prophesy the
actions of a whisky-sodden maniac.

Mounted men—Hump's ragged pony-riders—dashed out
at the horse herd from the thick brush flanking the meadow.
Yelling, waving blankets, shooting, they streamed against
the skyline like attacking Comanches. For one moment they
were howling demons bursting through the gloom, all the
startled horses strained up and point-eared. Then abruptly the
chaos: the whole horse herd thundering downhill in panic,
men running from the cookfire. The horses smashed through
the camp and came charging on, the roar of their hoofs
thinning the yells, shouts, shots. They formed a hurtling
mass calculated to trample to shreds any living thing in their
path.

Bishop and Red turned and ran, sharing the one thought
of reaching their picketed mounts ahead of the oncoming
herd. A forlorn bet. Two hundred horses were stampeding
straight down at them, and hadn't far to come.

They heard the horses crash through the dwarf willows
behind them, and they both spun around. Red squalled
and flapped his arms, while Bishop blazed both his guns
empty over the bobbing wave of heads. The horse herd
split before them, roared past, came together again, and
roared on. Their dust fouled the air.

Half-blinded, coughing and choking, the two men pushed
on in the wake of it, knowing what to expect from this
insane catastrophe. No hope of finding their mounts waiting.

35

Red's desperate laugh and flinging gesture put the final stamp on it. "They're gone!"

Where they had picketed there was left nothing more than hoof-scuffed ground. Their mounts had snapped ropes and gone bolting off when the frenzied herd came slamming through the dusk. Far up ahead the drumming fell to a splashing rattle. The horses had struck the river at some point and were churning across it, in nightmare terror of the howling demons.

With the decline of that noise, the descending night grew comparatively quiet. Bishop and Red stood listening. Scattered shots carried the news that the Mexicans had not fled far, if at all, and now there intruded the rocking thump and patter of riders racing down the open meadow. Mexicans, or the crazily treacherous Hump and his buffalo tramps, it made little difference which; they were all enemies.

"Goodby to our horses and saddles!" Red said. "And our rifles!" he added, swearing. They had elected to leave their rifles in their saddle scabbards, Bishop saying that six-guns would do for noise, that they weren't out to massacre the Mexicans—just to run them off and take the horses. "Hah!" Red hooted, remembering those optimistic words.

Bishop moved off fast, ears cocked to the riders coming from the meadow. There were times when a man hunted cover, any man if he had any sense, and this was one of them. The trees around here were mostly spindly, the brush thin, rocks too low. Hurrying, he smelled the Boneyard.

He sighted a tree, a big tree, black in the falling darkness, and reached it slightly ahead of Red. By the sounds closing up behind them, the riders had spread out in a hunting line. Taking a flying leap, Bishop caught a lower branch and hauled himself up. A weaker branch cracked, Red hanging onto it.

36

"Dead tree!" Red grunted.

They climbed up into it. Bishop heard Red swear, and told him to shut, the riders would soon be passing close by. Red was climbing higher, seeking a better spot.

"Hey, Bishop!" he whispered. "What the hell's this thing here? Look, there's another like it—and another. Holy smoke, the tree's full of 'em!"

Bishop looked up. He climbed higher and looked again. He examined a long, blanket-wrapped shape that was lashed firmly onto a pole platform between two branches. Above him were others.

"Dead Indians," he said. He plucked at the blanket. A piece of it, rotted, came away in his fingers and he flicked it off. "Dead a long time. This is an Indian burial tree. That's how some tribes lay their dead away. Didn't you ever see one before?"

"Not this close!"

Bishop grinned. "It shouldn't bother a body-snatching bone collector! You're right in your element, boy!"

Red stared at the silent bundles suspended about him, queasily, despite his talk of digging up corpses and selling cows' bones for fertilizer. Hanging up in a graveyard, as it were, was somehow akin to profane trespassing. Also, the grim relics curdled his stomach.

"I'm getting down out of here!" he declared.

"I don't advise it," said Bishop. "Here come those hombres looking for their horses—mad clear through and all weighed down with hardware, I bet! If you want to stay with the living, you better drape yourself over a limb like a good dead Indian."

They lay motionless on branches, close alongside shrunken and mummified bodies swathed in blankets. Riders dashed by below, wearing high-crowned sombreros and crossed bandoleers, carbines in saddle-boots. Mexican *hombres del campo*, a long way from home.

Watching them race past in the darkness, Bishop felt a tinge of nostalgia for the times he had spent in Mexico. These weren't furtive thieves, ready to cut and run at an alarm. A slight miscalculation there had put him up a tree. These were *guerreros*. He knew their kind. Lawless, sharp on the fighting edge, tougher than rawhide. They had managed to save their mounts from Hump's raid, and they were not about to scuttle out of the country for anybody—and the devil help Hump if they caught him.

Presently a clattering broke out, sounding like giants pitching dice, along with a considerable amount of shouted oaths in Spanish. Red chuckled.

"Rode smack into the Boneyard! Never pays to ride that fast in the dark."

The hoofs could be heard slithering and stamping on the smooth bones. In their reckless gait the riders had evidently piled halfway across the Boneyard before it slowed them. Being Mexican horsemen, unwilling to dismount, they lashed their horses to get out of the Boneyard in jumps, and then it sounded more like hundreds of slates being smashed in one grand pelting orgy.

When the din ceased, Bishop said, listening, "They're cutting over to the river . . . Now they've stopped to . . . No, they're coming back."

The riders jogged by, talking.

"Seems they know where the horses went," Bishop said after they had passed. "I can't make out why they didn't go on after 'em. Come on—we'll find out."

Red shrugged. "Okay, but I don't see much use in it."

They hurried to the Sandhole and crunched across it. A fringe of the horse herd had swerved this way and broken the surface crust. Boot tracks in the pounded sand would be hard to pick out in the dark. Some shots downriver brought them to a pause, and next they heard a flurry of hoofbeats coming toward them. A dozen long strides took Bishop to Crazy Chisera Rock and he clambered up onto the top of it, Red close behind him. They lay there flat with guns drawn. Red whispered wryly that now would be a handy time for the river to overflow into the Sandhole and sink those approaching riders.

The riders were some of Hump's buffalo tramps. They hauled in, and one of them got down to examine the sand. But it was too dark now for him to read sign, and he cursed and remounted. After some muttering indecision they rode back toward the sound of the shots.

Red wiped his face on his sleeve. "Guess they'll wait for moonlight. Or maybe till morning, if the Mexican outfit keeps 'em busy tonight. Man, did those horses run! Just like they knew where they were going, come to think of it. Well—it's farewell to *that* stake! You sure took on a sweet bargain, mah fren'! Just between us, and looking at it from a strictly business angle, don't you reckon digging sand—hiring it dug, that is—might've been easier?"

Bishop's eyes glinted in the dark. "One more reference to your deceased uncle, and you stand a good chance to join him in peace everlasting!"

He was not in good humor. This rampaging night had about wrecked all prospect of profit. Worse still, he was set afoot—a shameful state of affairs for a self-respecting trouble-shooter.

"Let's get off this damn rock and hunt our horses."

Red brought up a pessimistic remark concerning the hunting of needles in haystacks. "They're miles off in any direction 'cept up, and still going! Our saddles were loose-cinched and they've slipped under their bellies and—"

"You got a brighter idea?" Bishop growled.

THE MUSTANG TRAIL

Red allowed he hadn't, so they dropped down off the rock and headed in the direction taken by the stampeded horse herd, saying no more because their tempers wouldn't stand anything like argument. The moon crept up and laid long shadows while they trudged, and at last they met the river where it bent the trail.

The low bank was freshly trampled. On the far side reared what appeared to be a barrier of flat-topped cliffs sheering the edge of a plateau. But here the horses had crossed—as if, as Red had said, they knew where they were going. In the slanted moonlight the curve of the river ran a serene silver bow, disciplined by the north-side cliffs and the contour of the land. It spread wide, and for that reason it could be judged shallow at this particular spot. The horses had forded it, apparently without difficulty, and gone on up those forbidding cliffs on the far side. A very curious circumstance, considering that the horses were on their own, undriven, and in fright. Horses fought shy of crossing strange water.

Not exchanging a word, Bishop and Red unbuckled their gun belts, neck-slung them, and started wading across the river. There was a possibility that the horses had been brought to halt somewhere along the foot of the cliffs yonder.

Against the moon-silvered surface of the river the two men threshed blackly like bears in white brittle-brush. A rifle spanged sharply down at them from the opposite cliffs, twice. Two bullets sprayed feathers of water before them.

While the echoes of the shots rattled up and down the river, Red floundered rearward to the trampled bank, talking aloud to himself on the subject of trying to catch two hundred horses that were guarded by shooters. There, breathing hard, he looked back at Bishop.

"That jigger up there is either sighting his shots too

fine," he called, "or else he's being charitable—which I don't believe for a minute! He'll get the range right, next shot! You trying to draw him out? It'll get you a bullet in the brisket!"

Standing waist-deep in water, Bishop held the black cliffs under dour inspection. He splashed onward a couple of yards, and quickly side-stepped. The rifle cracked a third shot that plonked narrowly to his left. He backed off, joined Red on the bank, and they exchanged stiff glances.

"I spotted his flash that time!" Bishop said. His voice was low and wicked. "You keep him busy while I go after him!"

"Won't he shift his perch?"

"Maybe. Keep him busy, I said. Use your gun once in a while. If that won't bring him, try stepping out in the river. Make him shoot at you!"

"Be a target for him, huh? You're right generous with mah hide, Mistah Bishop!"

Bishop shrugged. "Don't know about you, but I aim to get hold of a good horse before morning, and yonder's the only place round here to get one. We know that's where they went. Quit if you want to—and tomorrow you'll be a dead duck!"

He slipped off and vanished along the bank of the river, leaving Red alone to think it over. If Red Delaney decided to pull out and take his slim chances on foot, all right; he—Bishop—was ready to go it on his own. By inclination and training he depended on nobody but himself, and any mistakes made were his own mistakes.

A fresh outburst of gunfire crackled—from the meadow or thereabouts, he made it. Hump and his buffalo tramps had stirred up a hornets' nest. Those soft-spoken, languid Mexican *guerreros* had certainly elected to stick around and do battle. Tomorrow they or the buffalo tramps, which-

41

ever crew won the upper hand, would be out to pick up that fortune in runaway horses. And they'd be hot after a certain troubleshooter, not to mention his redheaded Texas segundo.

V

Below the next bend of the river Bishop gave a minute to searching the night about him with his eyes and ears. The gunfire was receding, falling to occasional shots that were half-muffled, leading him to judge that the skirmish had shifted out of the meadow into the deep brush. One crew, then, was retreating southward, the other pressing in pursuit.

Up the river, Red's gun blared. Red was staying, inviting a duel. The reply was a rifle shot from the cliffs and the screech of a descending bullet. Fairly satisfied by it that the sharpshooter had not as yet shifted position, Bishop eased into the river and worked quietly over toward the shadow-black wall of cliffs. He hoped the rifle shot had missed Red.

The cliffs, he found after crossing the river to them, did not reach to the water's edge as had appeared from the other side. Nor were they as sheer. Along here they shelved brokenly and were veined by narrow arroyos. At the foot ran a beach of stony gravel, so low that most of it was wet.

He tugged off his boots and upended them, and for a while he squatted there, letting them drain. Red paid out another shell, and promptly the rifle chipped in.

Soaked, Bishop began growing chilled in the evening's slow breeze. He wrung out some of the water from his clothes and put his boots back on. His discomfort hardened his already violent intentions toward the high-perched sharp-

43

shooter. Buckling on his gun belts, he straightway set out to tackle climbing the cliffs. No doubt there was somewhere an easier route upward; he lacked the time to search for it, and guessed it would be guarded, anyway.

The arroyos were what made a possible task of scaling the cliffs. Rains of centuries had cut them into a maze of barrancos. They bent and angled, one into another, but always they webbed on upward. At last he crawled out on top, where he considered taking off his boots again for the sake of his feet. Climbing in wet boots was brutal. He scowled, predicting blisters. Damn it, Achilles—that Styx-dipped Greek with only one vulnerable heel—didn't know when he was well off.

A plateau spread out before him, an immense grassy plain, its eastern limits lost in a moonlit mystery of space. It surprised him. These river-edged cliffs were an escarpment, then, a giant step onto a high level of terrain. And the high terrain looked to be good rangeland.

Bishop sent a searching stare along the rim of the escarpment. He could pick out nothing worth noting, and had to wait until Red got off his next blind shot from below. Then he spied the brief flash of the answering rifle, and he marked that spot.

He prowled a wide half-circle to bring him around to it. The sun-cured little seed-stems of grama grass swished whisperingly at his boots, for he walked upright on the approach, sure that the sharpshooter's back was toward him. So he stepped high and softly, and came up in silence behind a figure lying flat on the rim, cuddling a rifle that was tilted downward at the river far below.

A smallish figure, this, but size meant nothing. Some of the deadliest killers were little men, runts. Possession of a good gun, plus speedy efficiency in its use, made them big. This one wore buckskins and beaded moccasins, and a cattleman's big hat. A half-breed, likely, brush-raised and snaky, thirsting to kill somebody for the satisfaction of it. Probably the spawn of some buffalo tramp, aping the ways of his sire.

Bishop stooped noiselessly over the prone figure. With considerable satisfaction on his own part he snapped a sinewy grip on an ankle. Like tailing a calf, he jerked upright and whirled the shooter upside-down. It fetched a terror-stricken yelp. The rifle went sliding over the rim to a long drop down.

"Okay, runt" he rasped, catching the other kicking foot. "You shoot for all the water in sight, you can have it!" His catch was light in weight, but it wriggled and twisted, fists hammering at his shins, until he swung it as a living pendulum, head dangling. "Sing up when you hit the river —so I'll know you got there all right!"

His captive pealed an unmanly scream. The tone of it caused him to slacken the swinging. He took the trouble to tip his head and bend a frowning inspection to the screamer, thinking it might be a boy that he was manhandling, some mean kid trying to make his mark.

The big hat had fallen off and gone sailing down after the rifle. Long hair swept the ground, unusual only for its fair color. Buffalo tramps often let their hair grow long, but it was generally of dark hue, either by nature or from their habit of wiping their fingers on it after eating—and they rarely used forks.

Besides the long hair, fair and clean, and the face, also fair and clean, Bishop took note of various other physical features and conformations indicating positively that this shooter was not of the male sex.

He released both ankles on the back-swing, muttering irritably, "All that damn climbing to catch a girl!"

The girl sort of rolled over to a half-sitting position on the ground, her arms stretched out behind her, staring up into his forbidding face. She began edging off as if to scramble up and flee, but froze motionless when he lowered a glance at her.

He was annoyed. He showed it. His feet hurt—the only tender parts of his tough anatomy—and he was robbed of venting his displeasure by the fact that she was a girl.

Red had heard and glimpsed something of the encounter on the rim. He shouted up, "Hey, Bishop! Did you get the son of a bitch?"

"It's no son!" Bishop called down shortly.

"What? Sun?" Red was confused. "Well, the moon's bright enough now to . . . Say, you all right? Seen anything of the horses?"

"Just a filly!"

"Huh? Hey, I better come up! You don't sound all right!"

Bishop sat down. He got his boots off. He retrieved a cigar from his hat, where he had placed it to keep dry while crossing the river, and lit it.

The girl watched him. She was attempting to pull herself together, and had so far succeeded to the extent that her teeth didn't chatter with her trembling. But she failed to respond when Bishop—the wire of his temper relaxing under the soothing influence of barefoot comfort and strong tobacco—commented to her that maybe moccasins had their good points. He would wear moccasins if ever he had to make a habit of wading rivers and climbing cliffs, which the Lord forbid.

About the time the cigar was a stub and the unlovely feet were reshod, Red showed up. Red came hurrying along the rim, wet and dirty and in a foul humor, and at once he snarled at the small person who sat facing Bishop. "Damn you, I'll whip your—!" And then, seeing closer and more clearly—"H'm?"

The girl sprang to her feet. In the moonlight she was a

46

sudden flare of color, her hair a flung-back stream of polished bronze, her eyes blazing, taut indignation and dignity
in every line of her firmly rounded figure.

"You will *what?*" She actually advanced on Red. "Why,
you filthy horse thief! Get off my ranch!"

She hadn't talked like that to Bishop, who had all but
tossed her into the river. Hadn't spoken a word to him.

"You foul-mouthed ruffian!" she called Red.

Bishop liked her for that, liked her dignity. She had, he
began to see, her good points. On second glance he up-
graded her points to excellent. Taking upon himself the role
of referee, he rebuked Red Delaney severely: "Watch your
language, feller! This young lady's a—hum—young lady.
Not the kind you're used to being around!"

To the girl he confided blandly, "He's just a roughneck
who doesn't know any better. Comes by it naturally—his
favorite uncle got killed over a woman who wasn't any better than she should be. I give you my personal guarantee
I won't let him get near you."

Inasmuch as Red Delaney was now shying off from her
like an abashed stripling at his first box-lunch social, the
guarantee was unnecessary. Still it rang a chivalrous note
of fine old Southern gallantry; and Red did look rough,
unshaven as he was. Rogue Bishop was no more a Southern gentleman than he was a Chinese mandarin, but he
knew the rules.

"Sorry!" Red gulped. "Beg your pardon, ma'am!" He being a Texan of Southern extraction, apology was instinc-
tive to him when a female of whatever degree was involved.
"I—I didn't expect to find a lady up here!"

"You didn't," Bishop assured him. "I did."

"B-but what's a lady doing here?"

"That," Bishop chided, "is an intimate question, one that
I haven't been so uncouth as to ask. But now that you've

brought it up . . ." He paid the girl a courtly bow. "Permit me—I am Mr. Rogate Bishop. This roughneck calls himself Delaney. It may be his right name, for all I know. I picked him up in a barroom. We are looking for our horses, Miss—ah—"

"Donavon," she supplied. Something in the big man's tone, or his manner, brought her to add, "Sera Donavon."

"Sarah?" Red took it up brightly, anxious to redeem himself and prove he was human. "Well, now, that was the name of another uncle of mine's favorite wife. My favorite, I mean. His fourth wife. She was the cutest little button that ever was."

He was about to go on and splice that coincidence into a happy knot of mutual regard, but the girl cut him off.

"No," she corrected him coldly. "Not Sarah—I don't like that name. My name is Sera. S-e-r-a. Do you know your letters? Mr. Bishop does, I'm sure. Please explain it to your man, Mr. Bishop, will you?"

"I don't know that I could get it through his thick head," said Bishop. "He's ignorant in English, let alone Spanish names."

"My name isn't really Spanish," she told him. "Sera is short for Chisera. It's Indian."

"Huh?" Red blurted. "*Chisera!*"

The blank silence that followed was broken by Bishop. "My ignorant and illiterate hired man is thinking you're up on the wrong rock," he explained to the girl, watching her face. "Also, he thinks you're not—ah—dressed according to specifications. He's got a one-track mind that runs to young and undraped witches. Takes after his uncle."

Sera Donavon evidently knew the lurid legend of Crazy Chisera Rock. Her face crimsoned. She said with sedate distinctness, "My parents didn't know the Indian meaning of the name, when they gave it to me. They thought it a pretty name. I shortened it after I learned it was Indian for 'witch.'"

"And so," Bishop suggested, "that left you only a little bit of a witch!" The glint of humor in his eyes made the remark acceptable. He asked in the same moderate and slightly ironic tone, "Do you as a general rule shoot at strangers? We're hunting for our runaway horses. Those were scare-off shots you banged away at us, though it wouldn't surprise me if you could've hit us. They came close."

"I can shoot," she agreed quietly. "My father taught me, after we settled here. I thought you belonged with a gang of buffalo tramps I've seen skulking down below. If your horses are with the others that came on over a while ago, they won't stray far."

"The horses came up here?" Bishop asked.

"Yes. There's a road up—I was guarding it. What was all that shooting down along the river? That was what brought me out on guard. Did those buffalo tramps make trouble?"

"Some," Bishop said, and changed the subject, sending Red a rapid glance. "What kind of outfit have you got up here?"

"Don't you know?" Sera Donavon showed some surprise. "Weren't you told? I should have thought—"

"We didn't get much time for talking, before the horses stampeded. And less after it started." Bishop surmised that she took it for granted that he and Red were acquainted with the Mexicans and had come from their camp. He wondered about that.

She nodded, taking his glib explanation at face value. "I see. Why, this is a horse ranch. My father and I came here from Valverde after my mother died."

"I knew you were a Texan," Red put in, trying again to win favor. "So'm I."

THE MUSTANG TRAIL

It didn't get him far. "Texans," she observed, "are like most people anywhere—some good, some bad." Her look placed him in the worst category. "My father was one of the best. And a good horseman."

Bishop caught the past tense. He asked, "What brought him to settle here? I see it's good range, but it's a long way from anywhere."

"That was the reason," she answered him. "Almost any trail outfit, by the time it has traveled this far, will have a few sick or worn-out horses in the remuda. My father traded for them, and with time and patience he put them back into sound shape. Some, he sold. The best, he kept— the big horses, solid color. He worked hard. There'd come a time, he believed, when his horses would be in demand at top prices, as Army remounts."

"Smart head on him!" Red commended heartily. "What I did, I crossed good stock with picked broncs, and got—"

"Snub it, mustanger!" Bishop interrupted. To him, a horse represented a convenient means of getting from here to yonder when such getting was called for. He wasn't interested in the breeding and training of the animal. It required hard work and a world of patience—two elements of small value in his fast life. He put a question to the girl. "Where's your father now?"

"He's dead," she answered. "Thieves ambushed him last fall, when he took some horses up the trail to sell. They killed him. He was—a good man."

Bishop inclined his head and touched his hat, willing to grant that the unfortunate Mr. Donavon had been a good man within his scope. "So both your parents have passed on to a better world," he pronounced gravely, thinking of big horses, solid color, broken to saddle, at one hundred and twenty-five dollars per head on delivery, clear title. "You got a crew?"

"I had five Cherokee men. They were good hands with the horses. This spring I didn't have enough money left to go on paying them, so I had to let them go. I'm not the horse trader my father was," Sera Donavon added ruefully. Then brightening, "But I have a fortune in good horses, if I can get them up to Fort Griffin!"

"Good Lord, girl!" Red burst out. "Are you saying you're here all alone in the wilds?" He was honestly horrified, stricken to the core by her predicament and its hair-raising risks. "What a spot for a girl to be in! It's—it's scandalous!"

She looked at him. Crisply, she retorted, "To be alone is hard for me—but at least I don't have to put up with rough talk and bad manners!"

"And that means you!" murmured Bishop to Red. "Button up your mug—I'm handling this!" To Sera Donavon, he said, "No, my dear Miss Donavon, you don't have to put up with that, not from anybody. I'll see to it he behaves himself!"

"Thank you, Mr. Bishop," she said.

The expression on Red's face betrayed his burning indignation. He had been raised on the tradition of punctilious respect toward all womenkind, and for this particular member of it he was rapidly developing a special consideration. It galled him to find himself playing the part of bad dog-in-leash to a notorious hardcase whose designs on the girl, he darkly suspected, were as sinister as those of a lobo stalking a lamb. There wasn't a thing he could think of to do about bettering the situation, either. Rogue Bishop had won the inside track and was playing it for all it was worth.

Under Bishop's deceptively idle questioning, Sera Donavon let it be known that the Donavon horse ranch was blessed with a nearly perfect location. Down the river there was a passable road leading up onto the grassed plateau. The river there ran deep. You had to cross hereabouts at the shallow ford, then follow down the strip of gravel beach to the foot of the road. The Donavon house stood at the top of it.

Sera's father had known what he wanted, and he had found it—dependable grass and water, the range so located that it could easily be guarded from the thieving brush-thugs and outlaws who roamed the trail. About the only event he had failed to provide against was his own sudden death.

VI

Despite Sera Donavon's glowing description of the ranch, and her protest that to be alone on it was preferable to certain other alternatives, Bishop sensed a wistfulness behind the brave words. She had to fight off her aching loneliness, stand against waves of despair when things went wrong, when the ranch became her prison, when life presented itself to her as a solitary and barren existence. There were, without doubt, nights when she was desperately afraid, as she had every right to be.

"We'll see you safely to the house," Bishop told her generously. "Those tramps down there are too busy tonight to cross the river. If any do happen to, we'll handle them for you. Hum—I'll appreciate, if you insist, some hot coffee and a fire to dry by. I'll take the coffee black. With a dash of whisky for the sake of my chest." He coughed. His chest was as sound as a barrel.

Red Delaney wanted the same. But he would have waited for a proper invitation from her, if it meant shivering all night. Where he was raised, men just didn't move in like that on an unattached young lady. He eyed Bishop askance, searching him for nefarious intentions and ulterior motives. He could get along with a badman, even get to liking him, but the presence of this girl—and her horses—canceled out any such masculine friendship. He had no illusions about Rogue Bishop.

And Bishop, quite aware of the trend Red's mind was taking, drew his wide lips straighter and said to him ever so gently, "Come on, Red, if you're ready—if you want to!"

Two meanings edged his offer. He—more blindingly sudden than Red—could revoke a friendship when it soured and dissolve it in gunsmoke if necessary. He recognized the distrust in Red's eyes, the rising challenge, and it was his way to meet aggression head-on for prompt settlement.

Under the chill stare, Red tightened up visibly. He sent a glance at Sera Donavon, to discover how she reacted to the tall troubleshooter's presumptuous self-invitation. If she objected, he would back her up, come what may.

Evidently sensing the undercurrent of sharp discord, Sera Donavon murmured a hurried assent. Although she displayed an aversion to Red as a roughneck, even she could judge that he was outclassed by Bishop. A casual fighter took his life in his hands, going against a professional. For all his cloak of politeness, everything about Bishop bespoke the professional fighter—dominant, calmly high-handed, tinged with the arrogance of efficiency.

She led the way southward along the rim. Bishop and Red followed, pacing well apart, each in meditative silence.

The house stood at the head of a steep road, as Sera Donavon had described it. The road ran up a deep and narrow pass that crookedly split the high escarpment. It was a comfortably large house, built of peeled logs on a rock-and-mortar foundation. As well as guarding the pass, it commanded a view of the plateau.

Farther back were some outbuildings—barn, bunkhouse, stables, and tack shed—and beyond them the horse corrals and breaking pen. The only difference between this and a going outfit was the unnatural hush, like that of a ghost town not yet falling into decay.

Bishop lit the lamps and built a roaring fire in the main

room. While he and Red spread out to steam dry, Sera busied herself in the kitchen. Moving over to peer in at her after a while, Bishop nodded approval. She was preparing not only coffee but a hot meal. She was okay as a hospitable hostess, willing or not. Engagingly attractive, too, though maybe somewhat on the small side.

A man could search far and long, he supposed, and do a lot worse. Yes, indeed. As the Texans said in their highest but understated praise—she'd do to take along. Definitely. And she surely needed a man by her, if ever a girl did. A good man to take her in hand and keep her out of trouble. Protect her. Guard and guide her. A young and pretty girl like that, trying to go it alone—damned foolishness. Time something was done about it.

He took his eyes off her, suddenly conscious that she was unknowingly inspiring him to muse along erotic paths. The pleasant smell of the kitchen, he guessed, had a bit to do with it. Most of the women he had known moved in a different kind of atmosphere. A clean kitchen had it all over a perfumed boudoir, when it came to arousing a man's imagining. Provided, of course, the kitchen contained a pretty girl.

Returning to the fireplace, Bishop found Red watching him. He grunted a blunt, "Well?"

Red made no response. From his expression, Bishop judged that he, too, was growing keenly interested in Sera Donavon's present welfare and future prospects. Keenly interested and, very plainly, jealously protective. These Texas brush-busters took an earnest stand on such matters. Blushing knights in shining armor. Treated a girl as if she was a fragile angel on a pedestal. Shrank from using forceful persuasion. Would pull a gun on any man who did—while likely that was what the girl wanted.

It might become convenient, Bishop thought, to clout

Red cold and toss him over the cliff, for the girl's sake. She deserved to be pursued without interruption, as a normal young woman with warm human feelings.

Then Sera came in from the kitchen to serve her excellent cooking, and Bishop took his mind off trivialities. She was a treasure in every way, a lonesome jewel in the wilderness, waiting for the right man to gather up, place in her proper setting, and enrich her life. She'd do to take along.

Morning brought a change in affairs.

It started with Red's hunting up a razor, one that had belonged to Mr. Donavon, and scraping off his rusty bristle. The instant Bishop laid eyes on him, at breakfast, he realized belatedly that he had underestimated the Texan's crafty resourcefulness.

He—master of trickery and the fast switch—had been dirtily double-crossed by an amateur, while he slept.

Red had washed and scrubbed himself pink, besides practically shaving to the bone. He had cleaned the mud from his clothes and boots. He had combed his hair and even cleaned his fingernails. In the morning's bright light he flaunted a slick freshness. Not handsome, but aggravatingly clean and wholesome looking, the dog. Anything but a frowzy roughneck.

With darting energy and fine examples of Southern chivalry and mannerly flourishes, he swooped forward and drew out Sera's chair for her, and alertly helped her to coffee and everything else on the table before she knew she wanted it. Astonished, Sera thanked him. She kept glancing at him all through breakfast, as at a personable young man whom she had met only that morning. Her glances were unobtrusive, maidenly modest, until Red caught one in a glance of his own. He and she held eyes. They both colored, and smiled for no sensible reason whatever.

Blasted caperings and cavortings, Bishop thought dourly.

By contrast to Red, in the pure light of morning he looked all too starkly what he was—a tough gunslinging gambler and troubleshooter seasoned with faithless cynicism and biting violence. Any day was wrong for him that didn't begin with a bracer compounded of strong black coffee fortified with straight Kentucky whisky, followed immediately by six inches of cigar, preferably Mexican.

This new day, bereft of bourbon, out of cigars, Rogue Bishop was not at his best. The insolent sunlight picked out pitilessly the furrows from beaked nostrils to mouth—the leather skin, deepset eyes, lean jaw. Hard features that the moonlight last night had kindly softened, as had the lamplight, or at least made younger and less harsh.

He ate little breakfast. It was nourishing food, he supposed, but who wanted to astound his stomach this early?

Finding a cigar butt in the pocket of his coat, he clamped it between his teeth and searched for a match. Red, breaking off a conversation, looked pointedly at the frayed butt, then at Sera. Bishop heaved back his chair, growled a word, and stalked outside to smoke, leaving Sera and Red engaged in an animated discussion that had to do with horse-breeding and related subjects.

"Oh, but look, Red!" (Already she was calling him by his nickname. That busted horse nurse.) "When you mate a Morgan to a mustang—"

Where in hell did the girl pick up such talk? Mate? It sounded indecent on her lips, almost lewd. And the Delaney joker encouraging her. Maybe it was a courting technique. This young upstart crop rushed things too much.

The cigar butt was cracked and wouldn't fire right. Chewing on it, Bishop inspected the outside scenery. Last night he had given it some approval. Today he judged it inferior to most that he had known. Not one roadhouse saloon anywhere from horizon to horizon. A forsaken stretch of wilderness, this, barren of anything in the way of decent civilized trappings except for this empty-handed horse ranch. Donavon must have been some kind of crazy hermit, to settle here. Life was too short.

After a longer time than anyone could reasonably spend eating breakfast, Red came out of the house. He went walking cheerfully around, whistling, getting on Bishop's nerves with his unseemly exhibition of perky exuberance. He finally strode off toward the corrals. Bishop spat out his chewed cigar butt and frowned at the house, hearing Sera singing.

Red didn't appear so sprightly, nor anywhere near it, when he came back from the corrals. Confronting Bishop in the yard, he muttered raggedly, "Something's wrong here!"

Something, Bishop agreed, was. He eyed Red meaningfully. Red, however, was not alluding to himself.

"Listen, Bishop! There's a couple hundred grazing loose up beyond the corrals. They're all colors. Duns, blacks, what-all. Our two are with 'em. Still got the saddles on."

"What's wrong with that?"

"Don't it strike you awful strange how that bunch of horses found their way straight up here? In the dark? They were stampeding—yet they forded the river at the right spot where it's shallow, ran along the strip of beach till they reached the foot of the road, and came on up it! And here they stopped! How d'you account for it?"

Bishop shrugged. "I don't. They seem to have known their way. Or they followed a leader who knew. A mare, probably."

"I wish I could believe it!" Red said. "That's not all. In the corrals are three hundred head more, all big sorrels, all wearing the same brand—small D on the left flank."

"The Donavon brand, I guess."

Red shook his head. "No, it's the Delaney brand! *My*

brand! Those are my sorrels she's got penned in the corrals. I told you how I got cleaned out by stampeders. I told you I was only hanging round Fort Griffin in hopes the stampeders would show up there with my horses to sell. Remember?"

Bishop remembered, and coupled it to another remembrance. He heard Red whisper wretchedly to himself, "Chisera! Could it be, after all, she's—she's—?"

"From what you told me of your lecherous uncle," Bishop broke in on Red's misery, "about the time he was allegedly lured to his grave by a nude female, this girl was maybe seven years old. A bit too young for such goings-on. And she doesn't look like any Pima Indian that I ever saw."

"Sure—sure!" Red agreed, glad to clutch at any ray of hope that shone upon Sera's innocence. "I'm crazy to think that way! Why, she'd never—"

"Still," Bishop said, "she might be following in the footsteps of that young Pima witch. In a big way. The witch and her folks only got a horse or two at a time. Maybe our little witch here has cooked up tricks to get horses by the herd. Goes in for it wholesale."

"How? She couldn't do it alone!"

"I guess she'd have help somewhere to call on. Not hard for her to get men. Women have headed gangs before."

Red winced. He wasn't happy, for a man who had just found his stolen herd of horses. "No, it's not possible!" he protested. "She's straight, I swear. Besides, she's Donavon's daughter, so—"

"So she says! Where's the proof?" Bishop shook his head. "For all we know, she might have pranced up here and dazzled old Donavon into falling off the cliff!"

That, Red's bemused look conveyed, was possible. He'd have dived off it for her, himself.

"I gathered last night, from something she said, that she's

acquainted with the Mexican outfit," Bishop pursued, privately enjoying a measure of sardonic amusement at Red's expense. "It was the mixed-color bunch of two hundred horses that the Mexicans were holding. Strange, all right, how they ran straight up to this range. How d'you figure your three hundred sorrels got penned up here on a hideout ranch where strangers are not welcome? Bear in mind she cut loose at us!"

"Don't know," Red admitted.

Neither did Bishop know. However, he took an indulgent and broad-minded view of the circumstance. They weren't his sorrels.

"Come to think of it," he observed after a moment of reflection, "we don't know that the Mexicans actually stole those two hundred horses. Chances are they did, but we can't be sure. They might've been handling 'em for Sera. Getting ready for a selling trip north."

"What you're saying is, she might be in with a gang of Mexican outlaws!"

"Those horses ran up here like they were coming home, didn't they?"

Red's shoulders sagged. "They did." He dragged a hand over his mouth. "I know the sorrels were stolen. Stolen from me, two nights out of Refugio, way south."

"And here they are."

"I wish to God I hadn't found 'em here!"

"You'll feel better after you sell your sorrels at Fort Griffin," Bishop comforted him. "If you ever get 'em there. Look for Sera to raise objections. The Mexicans, too, likely. Not to mention Hump."

"You like dealing me misery?" Red muttered.

"Trying to be helpful. You might take a crack at bribing the Mexicans away from Sera. They could help you stand Hump off and get your sorrels up the trail with the other horses. Don't count on it, though. You know how they are about pretty women. First, it'd be better to take Sera away from the Mexicans."

"Take her away from—? You've got me all mixed up in my head! What d'you mean, I should take her away first?"

"Not you," Bishop said. "Me. Just to help you out."

VII

Sera came to the front door of the house and called to them sunnily, "Did you find your horses with Mr. Dreesser's?"

"Mr. who?" Bishop asked. The name rang a vaguely familiar note. He couldn't place it.

"Mr. Dreesser," she repeated. "Did you find your horses?"

Transferring his regard to a lone cloud in the brilliant blue sky, Bishop left it to Red Delaney to grapple with that awkward subject. Out of a corner of his eye he watched Red step slowly to the house. It was often remarkable, the advantages a man gained by simply keeping his mouth shut at the right time.

There went a muddled and sorrowful Texan whose tongue was about to land him in a stew. Any girl having the spirit to lie up on a cliff, alone in the night, planting rifle bullets within accurate splashing distance of unwelcome strangers, could be counted on to light a fire under any man rash enough to try outtalking her. The sorrels were Red's, but Sera possessed them, and in these parts possession amounted to ten points of the law. The obvious solution was to win the girl, thus regaining the horses with profit and pleasure, never asking her how she got hold of them. She was entitled to keep her secrets, like everybody else.

That course was too subtle for Red Delaney. He'd think it devious, not on the up-and-up. There went a cooked duck.

"Red! Is something wrong?"

Sera could tell by Red's face that something was way out of kilter. Bishop couldn't credit her with an amazing feminine intuition on that score. Red's expression was a plain giveaway to any eyes.

Red halted before her, on the ground, at lower level than the door. The rock-and-mortar foundation raised the threshold three steps, so he had to look up to her. His first error, Bishop mused. Leave it to him. He should have stepped on up and towered masterfully over her, replying in his deepest voice that nothing was wrong with him that she couldn't make right, or some such blarney.

Not Red. Right away, standing there below her, he hung his foot in his mouth by croaking, "How did my stolen sorrels get penned up here on a hideout ranch where strangers—er—h'm?"

"H'm?" Sera echoed.

Letting the lone cloud go its way unattended, Bishop searched his coat and found in the breast pocket a broken cigar that he had overlooked. He trimmed and lit it thankfully. This was a promising start. Now let the fireworks pop. Let sizzling hostility rise to becloud the underhanded trick of shaving before breakfast.

Doggedly forging on, Red said to Sera, "Our horses are with the loose bunch, yes. The mixed bunch that stampeded last night and ran straight up here. Yes, ma'am."

He was trying too painfully hard to strike a middle course, to be logical, if not neutral. And he was failing because his words lacked the trim of subtlety, his face was on fire, and he breathed as if he had been running.

"What I'd like to know is—how did those D-brand sorrels get here?"

The girl stiffened immediately. Her small figure filled the soft buckskin shirt. "Those are my horses," she answered quietly. Red's question was way out of line, one that could rouse trouble between men.

Had she been a man, Red would have known better. He would have dropped careful hints, kept his right hand down, and given room for compromise and debate. Such rules of behavior somehow didn't apply here. Rattled, Red stuck his foot in deeper.

"Where'd you get them?"

Sera's eyes gained a steady blaze. "I traded for them!"

Somebody on horseback was ascending the steep road up from the river. The crookedness of the pass hid the rider, but the quick-climbing hoofs rolled loose stones and a bridle-bit clinked faintly. Bishop crossed to a patch of yellow-flowering chamiso brush on the edge of the yard, fronting the house, and sank onto his heels behind it to wait for whoever might crop up. Red was too flustered to hear those slight sounds on the road, and it seemed a pity to distract him from the splendid job he was making of skinning himself.

"Who did you trade 'em off?" Red asked, after a dismal pause. "That Mexican horse-thief outfit?" It was a sorry way to couch the query.

He began a stammering scramble for words that were less offensive, but Sera didn't allow him time to arrange them. The young mistress of the Donavon ranch was thoroughly mad now. She was brutally stripped of her softened feelings toward that busted Texas horse raiser.

From where she stood on the threshold of the door, Sera could see down into the pass. She gazed over Red's head at the man riding into sight around the last bend, and said icily, her voice shaking, "Mr. Dreesser will answer you for me—you insolent roughneck!"

Red Delaney was a roughneck all over again. He'd had a short trip to gentility, and fluffed it. Fine.

But in the next moment, behind the blooming chamiso Bishop automatically brushed a hand under his coat, muttering to himself, "Dreesser?"

He, too, could now see the rider on the road, and he recognized him, knew him of old. Knew him as a survivor, like himself, of the days when youth flamed bright and hot, when the game counted for more than gain, and reckless daring heeded only the fighting code of the even break. Not so long ago, as time went. It was the fast pace that decimated the ranks. The survivors still at large were now mostly bartenders, livery stable hands, taciturn drunks, drifters—here and there a hardbitten gambler, a gunslinger too wise to trap, or an out-and-out badman not yet hanged.

"Dreesser? Hell! *De Risa!*"

Of all the far-flung brothers of that wild fraternity, none could lay claim to a tougher or more spectacular record than Don Ricardo de Risa—bandit leader, self-styled caballero of blueblooded Spanish lineage, one-time rebel general, all-time rascal and ace gunfighter. He was thoroughly at home on both sides of the Mexican-United States border, and wanted by the law of both countries, from the Sonora-Arizona badlands down to the Tamaulipa-Texas valley of the Rio Grande. In most places, mention of "The Laughing One" identified him. The name appeared on dodger bills, along with various aliases that he had found occasion to use at different times.

Up the steep pass he confidently rode alone, as untamed as ever behind his smiling exterior—capable, Bishop knew, of gay subtlety one minute and grim suddenness the next. His slim and wiry figure was set off well by the elegance of his charro garb: short jacket and slashed pants, silk shirt, hand-stitched boots. It was a hardworn elegance, showing the effects of travel and weather and camps. Some of the silver brocade on his jacket and sombrero had suffered. But he could be down to rags and still cut a dash. He was a dandy from the original chip. Bobbing gently at his hips, the white bone handles of a pair of guns winked in the sunlight.

"Damn the luck!" muttered Bishop behind the chamiso. "No wonder those *guerreros* didn't scoot!" And there he paid Don Ricardo de Risa credit. Don Ricardo had the knack of gathering good men and making them into dare-devils who would stick by him.

Reining in his splendid black horse before the house, Don Ricardo de Risa swept off his sombrero and bowed low in the saddle to Sera. His dark eyes meantime measured Red Delaney, the stranger. The unwanted stranger, said his cool glance.

"Good morning, dear lady!" he intoned. His voice was a reverent caress, his speech mellifluous with its mere tinge of accent. His eyes glowed in frank tribute to her. "And such a beautiful morning it is. Ah, but the grayest day would shine golden by your presence!"

He hadn't changed, Bishop noted. He was the same as ever, able to build the commonest greeting into an extravagant compliment. The same whip-brained twister who could dazzle any woman and outwit most men. It wasn't surprising that Sera, so desperately lonely, had spoken of "Mr. Dreesser" in a tone of esteem as though he represented shining virtue in a wicked world. Evidently Don Ricardo had not yet seen fit to bare his claws to her. Hell knew why.

Holding his sombrero deferentially to his chest, he asked her, "Did the horses come up here last night?"

"Yes, they're here, Mr. Dreesser," Sera told him. "They came running right back up to their old range. But—"

"I do hope you were not too disturbed. We had some trouble at our camp—a stampeding raid by a band of buffalo tramps. If the noise of shooting frightened you, I can only beg your pardon. I was alarmed for your safety. It was uppermost in my mind. Compared to that, Miss Donavon, the horses are nothing to me!"

"This"—she hesitated—"this man is asking questions about the sorrels you traded to me for them."

"Questions?" Don Ricardo snapped, instantly the chivalrous champion of defenseless womanhood. "He insults you with questions? *Mil diablos encarnados!* What animal is this?" He bent a stern stare at Red. "Name yourself!"

"The name's Delaney," Red said. "I'm from down Refugio way, where I raised horses under my D brand. That mean anything to you? It should!"

Don Ricardo shrugged. "It means nothing," he replied. The shrug served a purpose, executed with the lightning deftness of a sleight-of-hand artist. His right holster became empty. The gun from it was in his hand, covered by the sombrero.

Red Delaney didn't see it, nor did Sera. Bishop, behind the chamiso and rearward of Don Ricardo, did. He grinned one-sidedly in recollection of that border trick, a trick that transgressed the fighting code. Don Ricardo followed the code, within broad limits, but he disliked Texans on principle and preferred to surprise them.

Unaware that he was pushing straight toward suicide, Red said, "Those three hundred sorrels in Miss Donavon's corrals wear my D brand! I never sold or traded off a single one of 'em, not to her, or you, or anybody else. They were stolen from me and my crew by a gang of stampeders on a dark night. We caught sight of one of the thieves crossing a ridge. We fired after him, but he got away. He was wearing a big Mexican hat—like yours!"

Don Ricardo dropped a glance to his sombrero. Behind it, his thumb rested on the hammer of the hidden gun. It wasn't at all likely that he intended damaging that fine piece of headgear by shooting through it. At the moment of his choice he would simply uncover the gun and teach the Texan how to crawl.

"This is a most serious accusation!" he stated. "You place yourself in a bad position, Mr.—ah—Delay. Words are cheap. You should produce proof. But you can't, of course."

Red snorted. "I can! Everybody around Refugio knows a Delaney sorrel. I bred up that strain. My brand's registered. In my pocket I've got the registry papers on every sorrel horse in those corrals!"

"In your pocket? Hem!" Don Ricardo's cough smothered the click of the cocked hammer. He was about to bare his claws to gain title to the sorrels.

"Yes, here in my pocket!" From his pants pocket Red showed the edge of a wadded packet wrapped in oilskin. "That's where you slipped up, when you stole my horses!"

"Let me see the papers!"

Bishop rose upright from the chamiso, drawling, "What size hat do you wear these days, Rico? From here, that'n looks big enough to hide a cannon."

Don Ricardo twisted sharply in his saddle. His dark eyes stabbed at Bishop strolling toward him across the yard, coat thrown open and hands resting on his hips. With recognition of that tall, austerely garbed figure, he again made muttered reference to a thousand infamous devils.

"*Mil diablos encarnados!* You—Rogue Bishop!"

"Me it is," Bishop assented. "Got a cigar on you?"

A dark anticipation rippled over Don Ricardo's smooth face, and vanished. To meet Bishop on even terms required reining his horse around, or dismounting. Bishop wouldn't allow him to act on that first impulse, if the hands on hips signified anything, and he was watching the cocked gun for the slightest movement in his direction. Don Ricardo eased the hammer down and juggled the gun back into its holster. He flashed a smile.

"*Hola, amigo!* My hat? It fits me. Cigar? I never smoke cigars, only cigarettes. Perhaps some of my men—"

"Don't bother."

Neither of them made any motion to shake hands. They had crossed paths before, matched wits, and more than once clashed perilously close to a showdown. Old scores lay unsettled between them, forbidding the hypocrisy of a hand-shake, while at the same time each paid to the other a wry respect.

"You a horse trader now, Rico?" Bishop asked companionably.

"Oh, I deal in horses once in a while," answered Don Ricardo, matching the friend-to-friend note. "You remember my liking for good horses."

"I sure do. How's business with you?"

"Fair. Just fair." Don Ricardo began a high shrug that was meant to be deprecating. He stopped it, seeing Bishop's fingers spread, and carefully replaced the sombrero on his sleek head. "I pick up a modest profit here and there."

"You should do better than that," Bishop said reflectively, "considering you never paid cash for a horse in your life —nor for anything else, if you could help it! What's the deal here?"

Red Delaney, for once, used his head and kept quiet, tardily aware that he had all but run himself up a stump by letting it be known that in his pocket he held negotiable title to the sorrels. He had got a glimpse of the gun as Don Ricardo slipped it back into its holster.

Sera looked ready to spring loyally to the defense of the maligned Mr. Dreesser, the Latin gentleman of faultless manners and warm charm. Her wrathful eyes said that her fervent hope was that Mr. Dreesser could hold his own in this uncouth company.

Mr. Dreesser could. By guile and gunsmoke he had held his own and got out of more fantastic scrapes than Sera ever could dream existed. He chose guile now for a beginning.

"Rogue Bishop, you insult me!" he protested painedly. "You judge me by yourself—by your own low principles! True, I have had some slight acquaintance with you," he went on, understating the truth by a long stretch. "In my life I have had to meet all sorts of ruffianly persons. But I remain a man of honor and—"

"Snub it off, Rico!" Bishop rudely interrupted him. "Hell, I know you! I know the deal you pulled here! You had the sorrels that you took off Delaney, but up at Fort Griffin you found you couldn't sell for full price without showing title. You tipped your hand to Major Jennisk. He offered you twenty-five dollars a head, and you spat in his eye."

Don Ricardo raised an eyebrow. "You know that, eh?"

Bishop nodded. "So you came back down here and traded the sorrels off for horses you *could* sell for full price. The old switch!" He turned to Sera. "And you fell for it!"

The girl blazed at him, "You don't know what you're talking about, you—you gunman! I traded my two hundred horses for Mr. Dreesser's three hundred. A good trade! My father would have been proud of me!"

"That," said Bishop, "I doubt—unless your father was as trustful as you. Why did this joker trade with you, at a loss to himself of a hundred horses, did he say? He must have given you some reason that you swallowed whole."

"Yes, he did," Sera replied. "It was because the sorrels have white stockings, and he was sure that the Army would buy only solid-color horses."

Red spoke up. "White stockings don't count against solid

color, with Army remounts. Any horse dealer can tell you that."

"I know it," Sera flung at him. "I told him so. But he was sure he was right. So we traded."

"And you figure it was a clear gain to you of a hundred horses." Bishop wagged his head. "Rico, that was low! You took advantage of her womanly instinct for a bargain. You traded her the three hundred stolen sorrels, without title —or some kind of flimsy title you wrote yourself—for two hundred horses you could sell on a perfectly sound bill. This poor little lone girl. Rico, that's cheating! Low-down cheating!"

Glaring at him, Don Ricardo inquired, "And who are you, Rogue Bishop, to be calling—"

"It's a shame!" continued Bishop. "You'd sell her horses and pocket the money. Then, if I know you, back you'd come for those sorrels—and for her, too! You border-jumping buzzard, you'll never learn that honesty is the best policy."

"Have you learned that?" Don Ricardo asked surprisedly.

"We-ell, I've been hearing about it," Bishop hedged. "Kindly hold your horse still, will you?"

"My horse doesn't like you and your Texan friend."

"Then teach it better manners, or get off!"

VIII

DON RICARDO tightened rein on his black horse, which he had been unobtrusively kneeing, trying for position. He spoke to Sera. He exerted his gift of eloquence, while his air of injured innocence was that of a long-suffering saint patiently defending himself from martyrdom.

"Dear lady, have I not behaved toward you as an honorable man in every way? Surely your opinion of me is not shaken by the slander of scoundrels! Look at them—a notorious gunfighter and a saddle tramp! Look at me! It is their word against mine!"

On the surface, the comparison did reveal considerable disparity. At his best, in a clear light Bishop somewhat resembled a fallen priest who inspected paths of profligacy for rakish purposes of his own; and Red Delaney, shaved and all, couldn't pass for a Sunday school teacher.

Don Ricardo de Risa's slightly blunted features missed handsomeness, but his consciously potent charm worked for him, and he could put on a smooth mask of engaging openness.

"Would I trade off horses that were not honestly mine? To you, of all people?"

"You would!" Bishop put in. "And you did! But the deal is hereby revoked. The horses stay here, all five hundred head. Bring your men up to get 'em, and you'll have a

73

fight on your hands. We can guard the pass against any number."

"Right!" Red seconded. "The sorrels are mine, and the others are Miss Donavon's."

Don Ricardo split a thoughtful look between them. One of the few sins he had never been charged with was lack of nerve. But he wasn't in a winning spot for a showdown, by far. On foot, poised ready, Bishop could shade him. And there was Red Delaney to consider.

"There is a connection, I think," he murmured, "between this threat and last night's stampede! I should have guessed it at once, finding you here, Rogue. Those buffalo tramps, raiding my camp—you were behind it, eh?"

"Yeah, only it didn't go off the way I planned. Seems to've turned out pretty well, though."

"So you are taking a flyer in the horse-dealing game, too? Yes, I might have known it. Wherever fast money is to be made, there you will find Rogue Bishop!"

"And Rico de Risa!"

"Major Jennisk put you onto me?"

"That's right. I didn't know it was you, Rico. Makes no difference. These things happen."

Don Ricardo nodded. "Yes, it has happened before." He betrayed no anger, and for that reason Bishop watched him the more closely. Their eyes locked. Between them, each recognized the same thought.

Five hundred acceptable remounts for the Army. A hundred and twenty-five dollars a head, sound title. On this isolated outfit that was a derelict ship without a crew. Owners: one slip of a girl, one penniless Texan, neither of them possessing the means to get the horses up the trail to Fort Griffin.

Over sixty thousand dollars in horseflesh. High stakes.

And more than that. Aside from gain, there was the

challenge. It shuttled between them, the cutthroat rivalry, hard pride, remembrance of past scores, and the silent resolve of each to beat the other.

Red Delaney saw the steady stare, interpreted it, and his face thinned and he shot a look at Sera. He knew what happened when professionals like these two clashed in feud, and knew the consequences. The challenge seemed to create a complete change in such men. They could be easygoing, quiet-spoken men, comfortable to get along with—and then smiling a chill savagery, blind to all else but the concentrated dedication to smash the enemy who by some sign, perhaps unnoticed by others, had flashed the dare.

And if money or a woman was involved, the victor gathered up his winnings, his token of triumph. God help any surviving contenders who tried to claim it. A lobo disputing its prey was a kitten by contrast.

Don Ricardo turned back to Sera. "Miss Donavon, am I to be robbed of my horses by these ruffians? Here on your ranch? I appeal to you! Let me prove that the sorrels I traded to you were honestly mine."

Sera, the unwitting umpire in a deadly game, said quickly, "Of course, Mr. Dreesser, you have every right to! These two men—they don't belong here at all! Until they crossed the river last night they were strangers to me." She sent Red a scorching glance. "Unwelcome strangers!"

Holding a wary eye on Bishop's hands, Don Ricardo legged down off his horse. Although not tall, by his slimness and agile grace he made up for his lack of height. He bowed to Sera like a plumed cavalier before royalty.

"Then let us go to the corrals, where I will give you proof. May I offer you my horse to ride? He is quite gentle with ladies."

"I don't mind walking there."

"No, no—your little feet . . . Permit me."

"Thank you." She took the reins and let him help her gallantly up onto the silver-mounted saddle. Docile as a pet pony, the black horse circled around and high-stepped daintily under Sera's touch, Don Ricardo pacing alongside, Bishop and Red following.

It made, Bishop guessed, a pretty picture: golden girl on a big black steed, courtly attendant beside her. And two churls, as it were, trudging behind. He couldn't figure how Rico was going to produce evidence to clinch his claim.

At their approach, the sorrels threw up their heads and stamped restlessly. They were not yet accustomed to this place, and were penned in the corrals to keep them from straying, but soon they would have to be let out. Farther on, the mixed bunch of two hundred horses grazed out loosely, ears pricked, nervously alert after last night's scare.

"What's your proof, Rico?" Bishop inquired. "I doubt if even you can talk these sorrels into signing an affidavit. Are you bluffing?"

Don Ricardo climbed nimbly into the biggest of the corrals, that held about a hundred sorrels. "You will see!" he retorted superiorly, yanking his sombrero down firmly and slipping tight the silver concha connecting the chin strings.

"See what?"

"I train my horses to obey me—me, and nobody else. When I whistle, they come. Watch the sorrels when I whistle. That will be my proof. Watch them!"

Bishop watched, curious. He recalled that Rico did in fact have a wizard's touch with horses. Rico's coaxing charm was not limited to humans. He had been known to transform an outlaw bronc into an amiable, sugar-begging nuisance, without breaking its high spirit and mettle. There were men—and some few women—who had that gift.

Even Red, his eyes on Don Ricardo, grew interested,

though skeptical. Sera, seated aloft on the black horse, simply displayed a smooth-browed trust in Mr. Dreeser's personal integrity, honesty, and all-round qualities as a gentleman.

As Don Ricardo walked across the big corral, the sorrel horses crowded uneasily out of his way, plainly suspecting him of smuggling a catch-rope somewhere about his debonair person. The didn't appear to know him from any other two-legged freak that by unfortunate mischance ruled the world. They split before him and ran around the corral, coming together near the gate, where they snuffed comments and inspected him hostilely at distance.

So far, no good. Bishop creased his dark brows. What in hell was Rico up to? He was making a fool of himself. That wasn't like him.

Don Ricardo pursed his lips and keened a thin, penetrating whistle. The huffy sorrels took no notice of it, except to spear their ears sharper in criticism.

It was the black horse that promptly obeyed the commanding signal. Bearing Sera, it lunged forward, cleared the pole gate effortlessly with inches to spare, and landed among the astonished sorrels there on the inside. The black was a jumper, a racer, a king among horses. Knowing its regal rights, it shouldered the sorrels aside. The sorrels scampered off on a round-the-clock whirl, raising dust. The black, Sera still hanging on, trotted to Don Ricardo, as obedient as a trained hound.

Don Ricardo whipped up into the saddle behind Sera. The running sorrels and their dust partly obscured him. He sang out in gay mockery, "You see how my horses obey me, Rogue?"

The black jumped the far fence, bearing its double but moderate load of slim Don Ricardo and small Sera.

As a clever stunt in horsemanship it was superb, but as a

tactical trick it seemed at the moment merely mischievous, an exhibition of defiance. Sera, apparently more surprised than alarmed, didn't cry out or struggle. The trusted Mr. Dreesser had control. He had taken the reins and snuggled a steel-strong arm about her waist.

The black swung to the right and ran along the outside of the fence, on a course that would bring it back around the corral if it continued. Red, swearing, ran to meet it. But the black veered off sharply. It passed behind the stables, then the barn. In full stride, it raced straight on across the yard.

Don Ricardo's purpose became suddenly clear. His laugh at Red made it clearer. Scraping to a standstill, Red plucked out his gun. Because of the fearful risk of hitting Sera, he fired high, a warning shot. Don Ricardo's laugh rang out again.

What Sera thought then of the escapade grew plain when she began struggling to free herself from the encircling arm. Her chance of breaking loose was fainter than that of a dove in a hawk's talons. Despite his size, Don Ricardo de Risa was known to have outwrestled Indian bucks on a bet. The black flashed past the house and went clattering down the pass. Red ran hopelessly on.

Bishop rejected the notion of entering himself in any foot-race with a good horse. His anger was bitter, part of it aimed at his own failure in foresight, but his feet had taken sufficient abuse last night, climbing up the cliff.

There were plenty of horses here to choose from, and a catch-rope hung coiled over a post of the drop-pole gate. The loose ones out on the range, his and Red's among them, couldn't handily be caught afoot. He took the rope and climbed into the corral, and after some dusty tagging around with the disturbed sorrels he got the loop on one. The horse at once stood fast, showing fair training. He led it out of the corral and replaced the drop-poles.

With the rope he fashioned and fitted a hackamore. No doubt saddles were to be had somewhere on the benighted outfit. He considered searching the stables. On the other hand, haste took precedence. A hackamore would do for now.

Red came sprinting back from the road. "She screamed!" he gasped. "I heard her scream!"

Bishop nodded, not attaching nearly so much importance to it as Red seemed to think it deserved. Naturally, carried off against her will, the girl would let out a pealer or two. Shockingly disillusioned in Mr. Dreesser was she.

Red snatched the rope from Bishop, leaped onto the sorrel, and took off without a word of by-your-leave. The headlong way he dashed down the pass, bareback and with only the hackamore, offered odds of five to three that he would break his neck.

"Damn!" Bishop grunted, picking rope fiber from his fingers.

From where he stood he got a glimpse of the black horse, down below and already across the river, streaking a southward course, Rico and Sera still aboard. Rico had a sure-win start, and that black was a lot of horse.

No pushing rush, then. You broke yourself for sure, barging bullheaded into the other man's play. Going after Rico called for wary caution. Rico knew what he was doing, the slippery cuss, and he had his gang of tough *guerreros* to back him.

Bishop investigated the stables, and carried out a saddle and bridle and rope. He caught another sorrel in the corral and laced the saddle on it, and hit the road down the pass at an easy canter. Before reaching the bottom he heard what

sounded like an angry shout far down the river, and a couple
of shots. Then a faint scream, and silence.

Red Delaney must have caught up with Rico, he guessed,
and got the worst of it. Rico had let him catch up. Ambushed him. Too bad. Kind of a middling-decent jigger,
Red, even if he was a hardshell Texan. Enterprising, too.

No discretion, though, where a pretty girl like Sera was
concerned. Lost his head. He wasn't the first, and he came
by it honestly. Blood would tell. His Uncle Wesley . . .

IX

FORDING THE RIVER, Bishop headed southward. He shunned the open trail, foreseeing as a certainty that Don Ricardo would be on the watch for him. The Don had succeeded in turning the scales at one stroke. Sera was the magnet—the queen bee. Carry her off, and the stingers came droning after her. By downing Red Delaney he won title to the sorrels, along with the Donavon horses. And by now he had gathered his men in readiness to spike the final clincher on his coup.

"That was smart work, Rico!" Bishop muttered, in bleak admission that the trick had caught him flatfooted. "Why didn't I see what you were up to? Snatched her right under my nose!"

The total significance and impact of the trick hit him hard, now that he took time to brood on it. Rarely had he been so effectively outwitted. Rico, blast him, in minutes had jumped from defeat to victory. He had the game sewed up. The five hundred horses were there for the taking.

After passing the Sandhole and Crazy Chisera Rock, Bishop continued on downriver and reined the sorrel carefully into the cottonwoods. Up ahead stretched the open strip of grassed meadow, empty except for the remains of the destroyed camp where nothing moved. His instinct for danger, whetted to a fine edge, would not allow him to be deceived by the hushed desertion of the place.

81

About here, he thought, was where Red Delaney had come his cropper, charging into a trap that was baited with the girl to lure him on—pretty much like his late uncle.

The trap was reset, waiting. Here were eyes, fiercely overeager, probing for him. He could feel the stealing search of them from the brush on both sides of the meadow, like heat, a rush of wind, an invisible force. They were too intent. No bait. Don Ricardo wasn't trying anything that obvious on him.

Halted, Bishop considered the prospects. Most men were right-handed. On the right of the meadow, then, most of Don Ricardo's men would likely be by natural inclination, their carbines nestled in crotches of the brush, prepared to deliver the same saturnine joke that they had dealt to Red Delaney. Don Ricardo's sense of humor was apt to take bizarre turns when his spirits ran high, and he relished the game of checkmating an enemy.

Bishop backed out of the cottonwoods, not knowing whether or not he had been observed. He reined the sorrel off to the right, butting a course to skirt wide around through the brush and scout the layout. His chances of jumping Don Ricardo from behind were remote, but he hoped for some kind of opportunity to present itself for him to build on. Anything was better than riding into the meadow.

A fur cap bobbed up before him, from behind the tangled cover of a woodbine-wound dwarf oak; a ratty old cap. And the round eye of the muzzle of a new Henry repeater.

Bishop drew and fired in a single swift motion. There was nothing else for it, the Henry rifle about to explode in his face point-blank. The fur cap jumped, the skulker whom he had unwittingly flushed fell into the dwarf oak, and immediately the surrounding thickets came alive with buffalo tramps.

He heeled the sorrel hard, knowing then what he had

got into—a creeping ambush aimed at the Mexicans. Hump must have recruited all the brush-thugs he could find to increase his force, and he had returned to wipe out all obstacles between him and the coveted horses.

Shots ripped from thickets of low barberry and currant bush. Scared wild, the sorrel swapped ends and took over from there. It smashed off through the brush and broke out onto the meadow. Bishop bent low in the saddle and let the horse use its own best judgment. The gunfire in the brush rapidly gathered volume. The open meadow was slightly safer, perhaps, at that.

He heard the solid tattoo of running horses behind him, and he hipped around, gun in hand to cut down any ambitious tramp who thought to clip him in the back. But the riders were Don Ricardo's men, streaming out of that ambush attack. Among them was Red Delaney, lolling half-senseless, his head gashed, a horseman on each side supporting him. And Sera on the black horse, Don Ricardo up behind her.

Bishop raced across the meadow and split the brush on the far side toward the river. There he fought the sorrel to a shivering halt. The black horse smashed in after him, and he sang out, "Can't you learn to watch your rear, Rico? They damn near got you!"

The riders came plunging in around them, staring hard at Bishop. Don Ricardo snarled at him, "Last night we cut them down to less than a dozen and ran them off! Today the brush is full of them! This is your doing, you—!"

"Wup—snub it!" Bishop tipped his gun level. "They'd have laid low if I hadn't shot one of 'em. While you set your trap for me, they were crawling up behind you. My shot made 'em spring their 'buscado a little ahead of time. It's all that saved you from a quick massacre, damn your ungrateful soul!"

83

"You shot one of your own men? Why?"

"Because he was about to shoot me, as any of 'em would! No, Rico, they're not my men. They're out to get me as well as you. Their leader's a crazy killer named Hump who craves to skin me alive!"

Don Ricardo narrowed his eyes. "I see! A bad split-up between you, eh? When rogues fall out . . . What is that saying?"

"Then honest men get their just deserts," Bishop finished for him. "Doesn't fit this case. Not an honest man hereabouts."

"You never spoke a truer word!"

Gunfire from the western edge of the meadow hailed into the brush. There was cover here, but no protection. "They've got new Henry repeaters and I guess plenty of shells," Bishop told Don Ricardo. "They're laying down heavy fire before they come at us."

One of the men bent over, grunting. His grimace was small and blighted as he fell from his saddle. His horse shied, and another man caught up its reins. Don Ricardo glanced at the fallen man somberly. He had seen death too many times to show sentiment over it, but this predicament threatened to become a wipe-out.

"We've got to make a move," Bishop said to him. "Let's break out of here, *amigo*."

The comradely term, given offhand, brought an ironic grin from Don Ricardo. It signified that he and Bishop were temporary partners, forced into alliance by the hard press of circumstances. Grudges and conflicting purposes were to be dropped for the time being.

"The river, Rogue?"

"And on up to the ranch, yeah—before they get the same idea. Maybe they don't know yet where the horses went, but it won't take long for 'em to figure out. We can stand 'em off from up there."

"If we get there!" growled ,a leathery *guerrero* whose blood-soaked shirt gave the reason for his morose pessimism. "That stretch of river beyond the cottonwoods—*ay de mi!* They only have to shoot into the bunch of us to cut us down!"

"We won't go in a bunch," Bishop said. "Two or three at a time, on the fast run. The rest cover for 'em. I'll start it, to see how it goes. Let Sera have that dead man's horse. I'll take her along with me."

"I think not, Rogue!" drawled Don Ricardo. "The young lady is my responsibility, no? She will ride my good black, in the care of two good men—you, Isidro, and you, Paco. Be sure she crosses the river safely, or I will have your livers! Two others will bring along the Texan—I have a use for him. I take poor Miguel's horse."

He slid off the black, leaving Sera in the saddle, and mounted the dead man's buckskin. Isidro and Paco nudged their horses up alongside the black. Isidro was all Mexican; he touched his sombrero to Sera and murmured a polite phrase. Paco, a rough individual who evidently didn't hold with any such fiddle-faddle, took the black's reins in his fist.

Don Ricardo's look at Bishop was brightly inquiring. "Ready, *amigo?*" His daredevil smile perked wickedly. "Shall we start out and—as you said—see how it goes?"

What Bishop thought of the proposed setup he didn't bother to say, and his expression showed nothing. But when, at his curt nod of assent, Don Ricardo chuckled, a baleful glint flickered in Bishop's eyes. Rico, backed by his tough crew, was being too blasted smart for his slashed pants.

Bent low, they forced their horses on through the brush slowly to where it thinned out toward the cottonwoods. The trees afforded them some further cover. At the fringe, though, there before them lay the clear ground to the riverbank, and after that the river itself.

Much of their course ahead could be viewed by Hump's mob up along the high west side of the meadow, and those Henry rifles had to be taken into account. They had ceased firing from the brush, so were either getting set for a rush across the meadow, or they suspected that a getaway was in the making and were watching for the line of retreat. Bishop and Don Ricardo halted to inspect the terrain, picking out every rock, bush, and hollow for its possible value, each mapping his course.

"Looks better than an even chance to me," Bishop said. "I'm going to hit for that bed of rocks way down yonder."

Don Ricardo nodded approval. "*Bueno!* Once past that, we can dodge out of sight most of the rest of the way."

"We?" Bishop frowned. "Pick your own damn route!"

"There is room for both of us. I'll stay behind you." Don Ricardo tightened his chin-strings. "Luck to us, eh?"

"To me, anyhow!"

"Ah, but if we both can make it, so can the rest. If, that is, those still behind can hold your friends off. And if your friends are not sharpshooters. They're firing again—hurry!"

"Here goes!"

They tore out from under the cottonwoods into the open, lashing their horses, Bishop first, Don Ricardo hard behind him. Within seconds, a shouting uproar raised the signal that they were sighted by Hump's band. The firing had increased, and now it hammered furiously in a solid wall of sound.

A bullet smacked the dished cantle of Bishop's saddle and screamed off. He heard the thin whistle of others, and he bent low over the sorrel's neck and swerved sharply to throw the shooters off their aim. Don Ricardo, following on the buckskin, swore. Bishop twisted to see what might be his trouble, and found it to be nothing more than a bullet-rip in the brim of his fine sombrero.

As they drew closer to the bed of rocks, the buckskin took an extra spurt and came abreast of the sorrel, crowding it over so that Bishop would have to swing wide past the rocks and give Don Ricardo the inside track.

Their temporary truce didn't cover the taking of such liberties. Bishop rasped, "Stay back of me, blast your gall —it's my route!"

"I thought you could ride!" Don Ricardo jeered. "Can't you learn to watch your rear? Make way for a rider!"

That did it; ripped the truce asunder. Bishop slung the sorrel hard back onto its original course close by the rocks, banging broadside into the buckskin, knocking it off its stride. Both horses stumbled. Don Ricardo let out an oath. A pro-truding shoulder of rock loomed up directly ahead. Bishop, barely grazing by it, called out, "*You* make way!"

Either the buckskin was running too disorganized, or Don Ricardo's pride wouldn't let him pull back until too late; or he didn't see the rock in time. The buckskin did as well as it could to surmount the obstacle. It clattered sort of side-wise up the rock nearly to the top. There, on a smooth spot, its hoof abruptly shot out from under it. Momentum carried Don Ricardo on over the rock, while the buckskin rolled back to earth.

Bishop sent a look rearward, mainly to ascertain if he had got out of sight of the rifle-shooters. He saw the buckskin scramble up and gallop off, empty stirrups slapping, losing a rider for the second time this catastrophic morning. That was an unlucky horse. He saw Don Ricardo sail down the rock head-first like a diver, and from the manner of his sud-den stop he judged that the Don landed squarely on his sombrero at the first bounce. His diagnosis proved correct: after his feet came down, Don Ricardo lay motionless.

"If his neck's busted," Bishop muttered unfeelingly, "he's cheated some hangman out of fifty dollars!"

Yet a tragic quality touched that lifeless shape sprawled on the ground. In its rumpled finery it represented a flaunting elegance brought low; a gay scorn of dull conformity, disciplined by death; audacity defeated by a stupid accident. It seemed less than decent to leave it lying there unburied, for thieves to strip, coyotes to gnaw, buzzards to pick at the remains.

Bishop rode back and reined in under cover of the rock. He reached down and grabbed Don Ricardo by his short jacket, dragged him up over the sorrel, and set off once more for the river.

Don Ricardo hung limp, arms and head dangling down one side of the sorrel, legs down the other. Then he groaned an oath as his head swung in unison with the loping gait, bringing his face in pounding contact with the saddle-skirt. He was only knocked out, and Bishop had half a mind to heave him off for fooling him.

By the time the ford was reached, Don Ricardo had got around to making feeble attempts to ease his position and save his battered face. Bishop dumped him off below the river-bank, in an agreeably soft couch of mud, and waited there for Isidro and Paco to bring Sera along. That was a state of affairs he meant to alter, radically and promptly, taking advantage of the emergency to improve his own state. It was a temptation to give Rico a tap on his skull to keep him peaceful.

He heard a horse running westerly away from the river. Something was wrong with the rhythm of his gait. Riderless, likely, or hit. Or both. According to all the racket, the planned retreat had become an unruly rout. Isidro and Paco had been given orders to start off as soon as Bishop and Don Ricardo tested the getaway, but it sounded like the whole bunch was staging a dash. And Hump's shooters were making them pay for it.

X

First to arrive were the two men with Red Delaney. They came slapping and slithering along under the muddy bank, having hit the river farther down.

"Those hairy devils crossed the meadow and drove us out," one said to Bishop. "Others shot down at us as we broke cover. We rode the gauntlet, truly!"

Red sat bowed, clutching the saddle horn with both hands, in a fog of slowly returning consciousness, the gash on his brow blood-clotted. At that, he wasn't much worse off than Don Ricardo, groaning in the mud. It took the two men a second look to recognize their dapper chief in that redraggled blob. They asked accusing questions while picking him up.

"He mishappened on a circumstance beyond his control," said Bishop, mystifying them. "How are your compadres doing?"

"They come, maybe. Some."

"That bad? H'm!"

They arrived two and three at a time, by various routes, and gathered at the ford, cursing over their hurts. Talk ran sparely to those who hadn't made the getaway.

"Pacheco dropped near the cottonwoods."

"My primo—Eloy—did not get much farther."

"Anybody see Morales?"

"Sss-t! Who comes?"

One last rider came rounding in, on a stumbling horse whose head threshed low in dying protest. It was the polite and tough little Isidro. His mount floundered down the bank, and he fell off, rolling helplessly in the mud.

"They come after us!" he said. It caused a general move to cross the river

Bishop got to him. "Where's the girl you were supposed to bring here, damn you?" He turned him over. Isidro's neck and chest ran blood. "Where is she?"

In his urgency he dropped his Spanish—forgot it—so Isidro, still polite, answered him in English of a sort.

"The black horse, he get hit. He run. Paco, goddam *bruto,* 'fore we ride he tie her hands to saddle. Then Paco, he get hit. I ride after girl. No good! Black horse, he run like sonnabeetch. They shoot me pret' bad, no?"

"I think they've finished you, *hombrecito,*" Bishop told him straight.

"I t'eenk so too," said Isidro.

The men were splashing across the river, taking Don Ricardo and Red Delaney with them. They had undergone a mauling, were heavily outnumbered, temporarily leaderless, and their spirits visibly sagged. Defeat didn't sit well on them, but flight to the high stronghold of the Donavon ranch offered the only alternative to a wipe-out. Two of them turned back and looked down at Isidro and then at Bishop, inquiringly.

Bishop said, "You might as well," and watched them pick up Isidro.

He legged onto his sorrel. "When your lady-killing Don Ricardo de Risa gets his head to working for him again," he said to them, "you tell him from me he's a stinking *ladrone!* His goddam caperings have put us all in the hole—especially that girl!" They stared at him and looked away. His eyes were icily murderous. "Tell him I'll fix him someday for this bobble!"

He was gone then in a hoofed spatter of mud, away from the river, his mind on the broken-gaited horse that he had heard running westerly. He was on his own, and that suited him best, as always. Essentially a lone wolf, company hampered him when the going got tight.

If the black horse was hard hit, it wouldn't run far before it dropped—with Sera tied to the saddle. Bishop cursed Don Ricardo, yet he couldn't lay all the blame for it onto him. A tricky twister, Rico, without scruples or conscience, but he never knowingly would risk letting any girl fall into the hands of Hump and his kind. Particularly not a pretty girl. He was too fond of them. Nevertheless, it was he who had brought it about by bolting off the ranch with her.

"Wish he'd busted his neck!"

Hump's vagabond bushfighters were advancing. They had spread out in a wide skirmishing line, on horseback and afoot, only delaying to comb every clump and hollow for dead and wounded men to scavenge for pickings.

Bishop angled sharply off, hoping to reach woods before they saw him and brought their rifles into play. Those new Henry repeaters had it all over six-guns in the open at long range, and the buffalo bummers could shoot if they were good for nothing else. Somebody raised an Indian whoop, spotting him. He heeled the sorrel and stretched it out. The men on foot began firing, but stopped when Hump bellowed at them.

The mounted ones came pounding after him. He liked that less than the shooting, guessing Hump's reason for wanting him alive. Half crazy though he might be, Hump possessed the brute cunning to let the fugitive rider lead him to whatever it was he sought. Hump had inferred that there must be a purpose for this risky dash from the river.

Diversion, then, was called for, to throw Hump off the track. Bishop changed his course, put a brush-covered hummock between himself and his pursuers, and from there lined out toward the Boneyard, intending to skirt around it. The sorrel threw a crimp into his intention by breaking its smooth run down to a choppy gallop, letting him know that it was going lame in the off hind leg. A rifle bullet had tagged it and the leg was stiffening.

Three legs were better than two, so said old walk-hating bowlegs. Not in a race for life, though. Bishop swung over to the Indian burial tree, last recourse, and looked back. Hump's riders had not yet rounded the shielding hummock. He kicked the stirrups loose. Riding under the tree, he dropped the reins, threw up his arms, and caught hold of a branch. As he plucked himself up out of the saddle, he booted the sorrel onward, and climbed fast. When Hump's riders came steaming by on the tracks of the sorrel, he lay stretched flat on a high crotch, sharing a platform with an ancient corpse. He didn't figure on staying. They would probably spot him when they returned searching, after they found the lamed and riderless sorrel, and up here in the elevated graveyard he had no more cover from their rifles than a cat on a flagpole.

Before starting to descend, he took advantage of his high perch to scan the surrounding terrain. Some of Hump's rabble, those on foot, had reached the ford and seemed to be trying to shoot their way across. He didn't think they'd make it against Don Ricardo's crackshots on the cliffs.

Turning his head, he swept a searching look for his best course westward. His eyes fastened on a patch of black, and he let out a breath, staring at it, grappling with the problem of how he was to reach it. The dying black horse had run only a short distance before it dropped. It lay behind a low outcrop of rock near the Boneyard. All he could see of it was a bulge. If Sera was there, she was either pinned under the dead horse or lying low beside it.

He was about to climb higher for a better view, when the bunch of riders returned from chasing the sorrel. They had the limping animal with them and were arguing over possession of its saddle. One of them, gesturing toward the tree, shouted something that went ignored in the argument.

That one was persistent. He pulled out for a look at the sorrel's tracks. He followed them to the tree, where he got off his scrawny pony to examine the ground. His Henry repeater he held canted close to his chest, keeping his bandoleer of cartridges from swinging out as he bent down.

Bishop sent a glance after the rest of the riders. They were making for the river, drawn there by the gunfire. They knew he had quit his lamed horse somewhere along here, and a few of them rode over the hummock, searching the brush for him.

The man below raised his head and noticed what kind of tree it was that he had got under. Bishop heard him give an uneasy grunt. Buffalo tramps and brush-thugs took on the superstitions of Indians without ever knowing the Indian reasons for them. He made to move on and inspect the grisly tree from a less intimate angle.

Bishop dropped on him. It was a fairly long drop, and he was no lightweight, but the buffalo tramp eased his landing. His boot heels hit the nape of the buffalo tramp's neck. What the pony thought about it was contained in an explosive snort; it bolted.

The buffalo tramp buried his face forcefully in the dirt and didn't move. He wan't breathing any more when Bishop dragged him into the nearest clump of brush. With the Henry repeater and the bandoleer of cartridges slung to his shoulder, Bishop climbed back up the burial tree to the topmost bier.

From there he had full sight of the Boneyard. Four of Hump's ragtail henchmen were poking about its edges, kicking bones over—bummers raking for measly treasures. Human jackals. A shadow flitted across the bleached bones. One of the four looked up at the buzzard that had cast the shadow. The buzzard circled directly above the low out-crop of rock. For a moment it hung, rocking gently, sus-pended in an air current, then a slow flap of its great wings sent it upward, as graceful in the air as it was ungainly on the ground, until it became a waiting speck in the sky.

Bishop saw the man start toward the outcrop, where the buzzard had betrayed the presence of death. And he saw Sera.

She lay huddled against the body of the black horse. In its fall she had apparently rolled clear, for no part of her was pinned under it as far as Bishop could make out. What held her there, down helpless beside the dead horse, was a latigo strap that fastened her wrists to the saddle horn. Paco, damn him, must have tied the latigo with an intri-cate Mexican knot.

To her credit, Sera wasn't treating herself to a fit of hys-terics. At least, she didn't vainly tug and struggle to free her hands, and Bishop couldn't hear any feminine screaming. Maybe the spill had stunned her. Then he saw her move her face, and guessed what she was doing—gnawing at the latigo. She was using her head, all right, only her teeth weren't strong and sharp enough. Needed fangs to chew through that leather thong. The outcrop of rock was roughly a three-cornered angle, shielding her on two sides. She didn't yet know of the inquisitive bummer shambling toward it. Bishop sighted the Henry rifle at him.

Hearing horses coming, he reluctantly held fire, watching the bummer pretend aimlessness to hoodwink the other three and keep a possible prize to himself. Half a dozen hairy riders cantered around the hummock, one of them leading the pony belonging to the man Bishop had dropped on. Rifles ready, they back-tracked the pony to the tree.

They read the signs there—scuffed earth and the marks of a dragged body—which Bishop hadn't taken time to erase. They followed the drag-marks to the clump of brush, and stared down at the dead man. Presently, Bishop heard them speaking together.

"Warn't no bullet nor knife! What in hell killed him?"

"Beats me! It was a mighty pow'ful *sumpin'!*"

"This broomtail's scared," said the one leading the pony. He looked at the burial tree, and spat. The others looked with him. "My ol' lady was half Kiowa," he said. "You wouldn'ta got her near this place!"

"Feared o' ghosts?"

"Feared o' guardeen sperrits! Big medicine!"

They eyed one another.

"What'll we do with him?"

"Leave him lay, he's . . . There goes Hump's yell for us! C'mon!"

They rode off, leaving unanswered the question of the man's death, half-persuaded to attribute it to an unseen vengeful power guarding the Indian burial tree. An Indian might have been more skeptical.

Wiping sweat from his face, Bishop returned his attention to the Boneyard. The bummer was nowhere to be seen, but now the other three were moving toward the outcrop as if on his trail. Sera's security was thin, getting thinner. She rose to her knees and began tugging at the latigo. Bishop shook his head, wishing he could warn her to lie still. Besides the cliffs across the river, other high spots overlooked the outcrop at long distance—up on the meadow, for one. Her movements would attract eyes and win her a bullet; or, if they detected it was a girl, capture.

Most of Hump's gang were congregated at the ford and exchanging snipe-shots with Don Ricardo's men up on the cliffs, but it was an undisciplined mob, stragglers slouching about as they willed and swapping bits of gear stripped from the dead. They would get around to Sera sooner or later, if only for the sake of the black's fine saddle. As for the Boneyard bummers . . .

Over his rifle sights Bishop watched them approaching the outcrop. The missing one of the four raised his head slowly above the spur of rock that formed the three-cornered angle; he had sensed the presence of someone alive behind the outcrop, someone who might be armed, and he held a pistol at eye-level. He stared down at Sera. She jerked frantically at the latigo, staring back up at him, and in gleeful amazement he rose crouched to spring at her.

Bishop fired and knocked him back out of sight. Satisfied with the Henry's accuracy, he levered the next cartridge. The three bone-pickers were fleeing. One of them had a limp that slowed him; he headed for the outcrop, his nearest cover. The Henry cut him short.

With detached observation and no compunction Bishop watched the limping man jerk up his head and hands and pitch forward. Too bad he fell so straight, his head toward the outcrop. It could provide a hint for an inquiring mind, a pointer to his proposed objective, a clue to the direction from which came the bullet that struck him down. The rifle was almost too good. These blunt-nosed .44 slugs hit like a sledge hammer. Next he would aim off-center, knock the target askew.

He did, and had to do it fast, twice, on a scarecrow pair who turned off to inspect the body of the limping man for.

possibles. They searched it, took weapons and trifles, and might have passed on unhurt if one of them hadn't paused to scan the dead man's position. He peered off at the outcrop. He spied something there that caused him to call to his partner, and so Bishop got off two shots.

The sound of the rifle couldn't fail to be heard. The salvation was that it would scarcely be noticed, much less located, as long as other Henry rifles kept thudding the same note and raising echoes along the river.

Trouble was, a harvest of defunct brush-thugs could be awkwardly conspicuous hereabouts, drawing notice, arousing strong conjecture and suspicions as to the why and wherefore. It might be supposed that they were felled by remarkable sharpshooting from up on the cliffs—but that left open the puzzle of why Don Ricardo's battlers should reach so far out to score, when their most urgent job was to defend the ford and the pass.

Nursing the rifle, Bishop kept watch, not only on Sera but all around. He was prepared to shoot any tramp who got near her, but if he fired while others happened to stray within close earshot he was cooked. He considered climbing down and trying to get to her. Faint chance of doing it unseen. If he caught a bullet, then *she* was cooked. He'd have to wait for nightfall.

Sera was once more lying still, gnawing at the latigo. She knew by now that somebody was taking care of her, guarding her from harm.

"Probably thinks it's Delaney!" he muttered. So often the wrong man got all the credit.

XI

IN THE next hour Bishop added two more to the score, after which the locality became avoided for a long spell. He could imagine word going out that some hot-shot, for reasons unknown, objected to trespassers around the Boneyard. Imagination also pictured Hump climbing to high ground for a survey and spotting the reason.

A burst of heavy gunfire roared from the cliffs. From the concentrated sound of it, a number of Hump's men had crossed the river, found the road up the pass, and met a hot welcome. The firing slackened off soon to sniping back and forth. They wouldn't try that again today.

Sera moved onto her knees. She wagged her head from side to side. Bishop supposed that her nerves were finally cracking, letting in panic, hysteria. Then he detected the top of a bald head edge above the spur of rock, and that explained her actions: she had heard that crawler, as she had heard the first one, and was trying to let her unseen guardian know. Her nerves were holding up all right. That was a girl to take along, damned if she wasn't.

The crawler, more cautious than the first one, only bobbed up quickly for a one-eyed look and ducked down. Bishop waited. The bald head reappeared farther along, near the end of the spur. He fired a shade low, purposely. A tiny puff of rock dust exploded. The shattered face lifted for an instant, gaping, and fell away.

Sera turned her head, face high, sending unspoken thanks in his direction.

"You're welcome," he murmured.

He reloaded the Henry. Its action was smooth, for a new rifle. This was the same kind of repeater as those carried by the Sioux and Cheyennes on the Little Big Horn, he'd heard. Issued to them by government agents, no less. For the 7th Cavalry, old single-shot Springfields; they fouled after half a dozen shots and had to be cleaned—in battle. That crazy Custer.

He lay waiting for another attempt, knowing there were more to come. The careful attempt by the bald crawler meant that it was now known that something below the outcrop of rock was being guarded—must therefore be of value.

They had the craft and cunning of predatory animals, more deadly by far than intelligence. The more protected a thing, said cunning, the more valuable. Material worth was the only standard they recognized. To the support of that shabby banner they could call up a vicious courage fiercer than the deliberate bravery of intelligence. Morgan the pirate had proved it. So had many a bandit leader—Don Ricardo, for one.

During the downsweep of the sun Bishop flayed the scalp of another crawler. Sullen great thunderheads roiled the eastern sky, promising a black night, a cloaked moon. Now came the long waiting, the sun diving into the west. Bishop's mood heavied.

His searching eyes kept reverting to Sera. He kept thinking of the good rifle in his hands, and how one accurate shot could sledge-hammer a person out of existence in a wink. No pain, hit square. His hard face grew deeply lined as the sun met the horizon.

He felt old, and sighed like a tired old man, watching the sunset streak purple shadows and gold clefts across the land. Cramped muscles and hours of strain merged to beat his tough spirit into a gloom of dull anger. He bleakly weighed his life and for once felt that he had misspent it—that he should have settled down years ago.

The sun bowed out, leaving the brief after-blaze in the sky, the earth in deepening veils of darkness; and then the rifle was useless, an encumbrance.

He gave the rifle to an ancient corpse, and the bandoleer. Maybe the ghost could make use of it in the happy hunting ground. He climbed down from the burial tree and Indian-crept toward the outcrop, silently cursing the stiffness in his legs. Nothing like a fixed plan occupied his mind. A fixed plan could hinder the advance to the dominant objective. His practice was to take advantage of circumstances as they arose, shaping them to his ends as best he could.

The dominant objective was simply to reach Sera before the crawlers got to her in the dark and dragged her off. His problems wouldn't end with that, but anyhow he'd be there to remedy her plight one way, or another. To leave her there alone, alive—it wouldn't do. The memory of it wouldn't do to take along.

On the dark ground the bodies of the dead bummers lay in lifelike attitudes as though relaxing at the end of a hard day's toil. For a minute Bishop relaxed among them, listening and getting his bearings. Their presence didn't bother him. Dead mongrels couldn't bite.

What did bother him was the sustained silence every-where. No sound came from the ford. For some time now not a shot had echoed anywhere along the river, nor from the cliffs. Even an ear pressing to earth failed to pick up any rumor of horses moving about. He distrusted the silence, the stilled peace of the evening, the illusion that Hump had quit and pulled out. Instinct rang warning of creeping purposes, calculated designs, unseen dangers closing in around him.

He eased on, taking a course that would bring him around the outcrop to approach it from behind, rather than climb over it and skyline himself. The pale background of the Boneyard, too, had to be shunned. Tiny sounds reached his ears. Flat on the ground, he paused again to listen.

Dammit, they *were* closing in. Those faint rustlings were not conjured up by oversharpened senses too eager to corroborate instinct. They were furtive, their direction indefinite, but they were near and coming closer. Drawing out a gun with noiseless care, hooking his thumb over the hammer, he went on. He passed the outcrop by a dozen yards and slowly rounded in on it.

His eyes were caught by two rocks farther out, on his left. They didn't belong in the mental picture he retained of this place from his day-long vigil. He frowningly studied the murky shapes for a moment before going on, wondering if his memory could have slipped.

Before him bulked the body of the black horse at the foot of the outcrop. And Sera, a lighter shape in her buckskins, gnawing doggedly at the latigo—as slow a process, Bishop thought, as sawing through a steel bar with a nail file. The length of his glance at her was no more than enough to assure him that she was there and alive.

Sera saw him then, a crouched shadow coming at her. She began a frantic struggle, cruelly taut nerves at last giving way. Fearing she would scream out, Bishop sent her a hushed command: "Be still!"

He felt the rushing shock of her relief. When he got to

her side she huddled against him, shaking, stifling sobs, like a child coming out of a nightmare. He drew his knife and cut the latigo from her wrists. While rubbing her wrists he heard again the faint rustling sound. So did Sera, for her body tensed.

He stared around. The two rocks, he could swear, had moved nearer to the outcrop. He leveled his gun at the nearest one, refusing to believe that his eyesight and memory were both at fault, and waited for the rock to move.

It whispered, "That you, Bishop? Don't shoot—this is Red Delaney!"

"Well, I be damned!" Bishop muttered. The Texan was a sticker. "Who's that with you?"

"De Risa!"

"I be damned!" Bishop repeated. A pair of stickers. They had sighted Sera during the day, from up on the cliffs. Like him, they'd had to wait for nightfall to get to her. It pleased him that he had got to her first. Gave him a proprietory sense. He felt young, uplifted, vital.

They crawled forward, draped in mud-daubed canvas. Their heads peeked out from under, giving them the arch appearance of shy turtles rather than two daredevils on a desperate venture. Bishop wanted to know what caused the rustling sound, and Red explained that they had padded their canvases out with straw to give them more of the rounded look of rocks. The straw stuffing made some little noise, Red allowed, but it changed their shapes from anything human-like. They couldn't have done without it, the area full of prowling hoodlums.

"I got here in one piece," Bishop mentioned. "A little dust on me is all."

"You didn't have as far to come," Red retorted. He went on to say that from up on the cliffs he and Don Ricardo, with the Mexicans, had watched brush-thugs get bowled over when prowling near Sera, and knew it was Bishop's work. He and the Don weren't doing anything useful up there after darkness fell, so they had come down.

From Red's terse account Bishop filled in the picture. That Don Ricardo should be here wasn't surprising; it was the device he used that made it exceptional. He was a slippery catamount, but he hadn't yet sloughed off the old code, not all of it. A matter of personal pride, maybe. And Sera was young and pretty. That helped.

Coldly bitter, Don Ricardo told Bishop he was lucky. "You didn't have to climb down cliffs in the dark and cross a river, and fool forty rifles—sweating under a load of canvas and mud and straw! No! You took the easy way!"

He didn't mean it in that vein, but he was smarting from the spill that Bishop had forced him into, and Bishop knew it and asked him, "Who made you turn into a rolling stone? Who invited you here?"

He received no reply. Didn't expect one, didn't need one. Nobody had made Don Ricardo do it. Nobody but himself.

"Will you two highbinders quit scrapping this once?" Red protested. "This ain't the time and place for it!" He turtled on cumbrously and murmured to Sera. A hand holding a knife wiggled out weirdly from where his head had been, only to discover that her wrists were already cut free.

Don Ricardo's poking head twisted, and he scuttled after him. Red was not to be allowed to grab any credit for himself. It had to be made clear to Sera that she was saved by virtue of the gallantry and brilliantly inspired leadership of Don Ricardo do Risa—not by an inferior follower who, taking cheap advantage of a pause for discussion, got there first with a pocketknife.

Above the rustling of Don Ricardo's straw-stuffed canvas Bishop caught a muted medley of other sounds. "Hang up, Rico!" he muttered.

Don Ricardo's head came around, inquiring, "What?" The straw and canvas over him didn't let his ears function very well.

"Shut up and listen! Freeze!"

When the straw ceased movement the outer sounds came clearer, recognizable. Now that it had come night Hump's hooligans evidently felt that the outcrop could be investigated without risking the unknown sniper's bullets. They compromised with caution by taking long, creeping strides, and not talking above the pitch of a mountain lion's courting grumble. Their progress couldn't be detected from full rifle-shot range in the dark, but from here they were within a stone's throw.

Red Delaney was an unmoving rock huddled protectively over Sera, who couldn't huddle closer to him than the mud on his masquerade.

Equally hampered, unable to dig out a gun for fear of rustling his straw, Don Ricardo hissed at Bishop, "Do something! This cursed canvas—we had to tie them on us! I can't get loose in time! Do something!"

"What? Hell—here they come!" Bishop cocked the hammer of his drawn gun. "Damn you, I stayed here too long gabbing with you! Do what?"

Don Ricardo rippled a Spanish oath containing a strong statement regarding Bishop's parentage. "Do anything! Anything to hold them off while I get rid of this thing! You can match Satan when you have to—I've seen you! Quick!"

"Match?" muttered Bishop. "Sure, sure—that's it!"

He fished out a match from his pocket. He thrust it under Don Ricardo's canvas, into the straw, scratched it alight with his thumbnail, and withdrew his hand.

"You better ki-yi for the river pretty quick now, Rico," he advised.

Results came fast. There was a sizzling crackle and a puff of flame. Don Ricardo let out an astounded howl and leaped to his feet. Fire, best friend and worst enemy of man, diligently torched the straw packed between his rear and the canvas. He bounded over the outcrop in a direct run for the river, tearing at the burning embrace, disregardful of the hooligans. Getting to quenching water was his only concern at the moment.

Sera and Red rolled over to see what had happened. One of them, or both, leaned on the gas-bloated belly of the dead horse. The carcass vented a loud and sepulchral honk under the pressure.

Bishop peered over the outcrop. It was a marvel, what disturbance a sudden phenomenon could wreak among the benighted ignorant. He had noticed it in some Indians who were not town-broke. These more-or-less white savages, shy of towns, had lost touch with anything more Christianly civilized than an occasional whisky roadhouse. Living as creatures of jungle law had sharpened their brute instincts, quickened their muscular reactions, but dulled their thinking faculties. Confronted by novelty, their brains boggled.

A flaming apparition, rearing up from the ground and dashing through them, was more than a novelty. Some of them ran howling after it a few paces. Others scattered. None dallied to cogitate on the source and meaning of that unearthly honk.

As an expedient in diversionary tactics Bishop was gratified with the results of the lighted match. He banged into Red in the dark, tumbling him, and yanked Sera up onto her feet.

"Come on!"

He rushed her off, half-carrying her to keep up with his long-legged strides, bearing a roundabout course to the river. Don Ricardo was still running his straight route, he saw, jumping rocks and plowing through brush that would have balked a kerosened burro. Nothing like fire to set a man's best foot forward. Pretty soon there sounded a splash, a hiss, and the fire went out. Bishop hurried Sera along in that direction.

Red, having rid himself of his straw-and-canvas trappings, overhauled them near the river. "There's a good spot to cross over, farther on down," he panted. "It's narrow and part hidden. Deep in the middle, though. Can you swim, Sera?"

"Lead on—never mind questions!" Bishop told him. "We'll get across. Damwell got to!"

As far as he could recall, Don Ricardo wasn't any great shakes at swimming, in spite of the many times he had crossed the Rio Grande, usually in a hurry. Don Ricardo, if he was still able to get around, would be searching for shallow water. Not the ford. Too open. Well, that was his problem . . .

"Step lively! There goes Hump singing out for blood!"

Hump's roaring voice profanely called the mob to return to the river. Running men could be heard snarling at one another, each vowing he would have downed that blazing booger if only he'd had a little help. They hadn't figured out quite what it was or why it happened.

Red said, "Here we are! De Risa and I climbed down the cliffs right yonder. We laid the canvas and straw on some branches, and kind of floated over." He reached to Sera. "I'll help you. Just leave it to me, and I'll—"

Bishop tripped him, shouldered him into a headlong dive, said, " 'Scuse me!" and barged straightway into the river with Sera in his arms. He had appointed himself guardian of an angel and damned if he would relinquish her.

Toward midstream the footing dropped embarrassingly away from under him. He had to let go of Sera, to use his arms to swim with. Red splashed up beside Sera, anxious to extend her his manful help and sinking himself every time he tried to do it. Like most riders of the Southwest's great open spaces where a ten-foot trickle counted as a river, Red couldn't dog-paddle six strokes without going down for a fresh start from bottom. And Bishop, fully garbed and weighted with gunbelts, did only a fraction better. They called it swimming.

Sera, transforming into a sleek and lithe seal in the water, flipped over and dived down for Red. She helped him safely ashore on the far side, and rippled back for Bishop, who had decided to hold his breath and walk.

On the east bank both men sat down puffing and snorting, while Sera—not the slightest bit out of breath—inquired with sweet concern for her champions, "Are you all right?"

"Cert-huh-'nly!" gasped Red. "That wasn't so t-huh-tough, was it?" He added that he was glad to have been on hand to help her across. No trouble at all. Sera thanked him.

With a stout resurgence of energy Red led the way up the cliffs. This, he explained, was a feat requiring much knowledge and experience of climbing, plus an unerring memory, not to mention reliable night eyes.

Sera agreed that it was so, for she had climbed this same shortcut many times and it was marvelously clever of Red to have discovered it in the dark. She followed modestly behind until Red clambered astray for the fourth time, whereupon she scampered nimbly ahead and guided both men up onto the plateau in short order.

They were soaking wet and uncomfortable, and their feet hurt. Superior masculine self-esteem was slightly frayed. So was Sera wet, but it didn't appear to discomfort her very much. Her moccasined feet pattered lightly, and her self-esteem seemed healthy. She was home.

XII

THE MEXICAN defenders, tightly on the alert, came close to blasting the three of them off the cliff before recognizing who they were. They informed them that the *ladrones* down below were up to something. Had the three witnessed that strange streak of running flame?

Yes, they had. Mysterious, certainly.

"We shot down at it."

"I bet that was a help!"

Don Ricardo de Risa had not yet returned. Had they seen anything of him?

Yes; Don Ricardo was engaging himself in matters of closely personal importance, said Bishop, and would show up in his own good time. Meanwhile, they were to watch the river. Don't let those lousy *ladrones* come over—they would surely climb the cliffs, apes that they were, and attack. Not so?

Verdad! Unfortunately, the thunderheads kept piling up, obscuring moon and stars. The river was a sleazy ribbon, difficult to see. There were places along it where the *ladrones* could cross unseen from up here; they might even creep up the road of the pass.

"We'll keep the road well guarded, and watch for any cliff climbers," Bishop said. "Better spit on your gunsights."

"Strange that Don Ricardo is not back. He is not captured?"

"Not that I know of."

"Then why is he so slow?"

"*Quien sabe?* He was in an all-fired rush, last I saw him."

THE MUSTANG TRAIL

And then Don Ricardo came trudging along the rim.

The Don presented a sad spectacle, scorched tender, half-drowned, exhausted from climbing. His rage sustained him. His eyes glittered at sight of Bishop's tall figure in the dark.

"You hell-spawned traitor!" he grated in Spanish.

Bishop had his right hand under his coat, ready for a fast cross-drawn. "What's the beef, Rico?" he queried. He was sharply aware of the listening Mexicans about him.

Don Ricardo observed his readiness. His own hands, swollen by heat and cut by rocks, slowly moved from the near vicinity of his gun butts. The moment of trembling balance passed, its cause added to the score that would have to be paid in full.

"Watch him!" he snapped. "This gringo devil nearly got me killed!"

"*Amigo*, those are harsh—"

"He is no friend of mine!" Don Ricardo interrupted. And in a brittle tone: "What's here?"

He wanted to know who the this-and-that Bishop thought he was, to be calmly usurping command up here. He tongue-lashed his men up and down for taking orders—or at least general instructions—from anybody but himself. His temper was wicked; he had suffered indignity as well as considerable pain to various parts of his person. The pain he could bear. The indignity was intolerable.

Considering that he hadn't been around lately to give any orders, his searing reprimands were not entirely reasonable, and some of his hellion crew angrily told him so to his face. These were thorny *hombres del campo*, full of independence, and recent events had stretched their high tempers. It wasn't safe for anyone, even Don Ricardo de Risa, to cuss them out as if they were lowly sheepherders humbly drudging for some high-nosed *aristo*.

114

"You shot down at me while I was running on fire to the river!" he accused them.

They retorted that they didn't know he was the flaming thing. And anyhow they had missed hitting him, due to his speed. A voice in the darkness murmured that they would try to do better next time. It was a promising start for a bad row, a mutiny. Don Ricardo knew it. He turned it off, giving a curt command:

"String out and watch the cliffs, some of you. The rest guard the road."

That, they informed him caustically, was what they had been about to do when he came bullyragging along; Bishop had urged them. It made Don Ricardo madder than ever, but he had to hold the lid on or risk complete loss of control over them.

"*Muy bien*—do it, then!"

Bishop, in favor of mutiny—of any upset that might tip the scales to his advantage—tried pouring more fuel on Don Ricardo's fire, hoping to make him blow up and alienate his men still further. "Better get some rest, Rico," he advised kindly, patronizingly, like a family physician to an old maid with the vapors. "It's the heat. You'll be all right after a while. We'll handle whatever comes up, don't you worry."

He recognized Don Ricardo's trouble. In the ordinary run the Don wasn't such a bad loser when the trick turned against him. He could give and take, and he relished a battle of wits. What he couldn't stand was being made to look ridiculous. It knocked out all his sense of humor. Also, being a confirmed dandy, he hated having his fine garb ruined. The flames had singed his sleek black hair, and even his thin line of mustache was frizzled. What the heat had done to his rear wasn't visible.

Ignoring Bishop's backhanded advice, Don Ricardo detained his men for a moment. He spoke to them with forced friendliness, patching up the damage, complimenting them on their doings of the day. He made a joke of their taking potshots down at him.

"You must have used paper bullets, which caught on fire from me!"

They moved away to take their stations, paying him a few grunts of laughter. He had created a resentment among them, though, that would take some time to erase. Worse, there now existed a spark of doubt that could flare up and destroy all their confidence in him. It was difficult for their kind to retain total respect for a leader who got fooled into acting the scorched clown and then pawed the hole deeper. He could not afford to antagonize them.

Red, missing a good chance to keep quiet, said, "We ought to turn my sorrels out to graze with Sera's bunch. They're not much likely to drift now."

Don Ricardo turned on him with malevolent joy. He badly needed an excuse to uncork his bottled feelings, and here was one all set up for him. A Texan, at that.

"Your sorrels? And the others you call Sera's, eh?" He spoke caressingly. "That takes in all the horses on the place, no?"

"Yes, just about," Red answered him. "She and I own 'em."

"Congratulations! And how do you—ah—establish that claim? How will you go about it?"

"Their brands are registered in our names. We can both show the papers to prove it any time, at Fort Griffin or anywhere else. I've still got the sorrels' papers in my pocket."

"Ah, yes, so you have. But the horses will be sold by me, all five hundred!"

"How'll *you* go about it?"

116

"Like this!" A gun spiked from Don Ricardo's hand.

"Y'know, Rico," casually put in Bishop, "it won't do you much good to shoot him for his horse papers. They're in his name. No use to anybody else, without a bill of sale signed by him."

Don Ricardo frowned. He disliked all forms of documents, and his knowledge of them was hazy; they were bothersome, unnecessary complications particularly in property transactions.

"Thank you for bringing it up," he acknowledged, sarcasm edging his tone. "The rights of larceny must have a legal stamp. Very well—he will write out a bill of sale to me!"

Red shook his head. "Why should I, if you're going to shoot me anyhow?"

"He won't," Bishop put in.

"Of course not!" Don Ricardo let his gun dangle. "After you write me your bill of sale—"

"No good, Rico! You could haul bills of sale by the wagonload, all signed over to you, and still run into bad trouble trying to sell horses to the Army! You cussed out Jennisk. He's an unforgiving sourbelly. You're in his black book. He's posted you as a horse thief. No, you don't sell horses to him —nor to any Army post in his division. Not you, Rico! You queered yourself in the remount-selling business, when you sashayed up to Fort Griffin and sassed that fat major!"

Don Ricardo stood speechless. The moon lobbed above the roiling thunderheads; its pale light washed his face to carved ivory. In his frustration he appeared tempted to go ahead and shoot Red and then take a crack at Bishop.

Off-tracked by another thought, he demanded, "What deal did you make with Jennisk?"

"I contracted with him to deliver three hundred remounts,

on a kickback that would give us both a profit. Your horses—
the sorrels, that is, that you stole off Delaney, here. As I've
told you, at the time I didn't know it was you. I didn't know
where the horses came from." Bishop shrugged. "If I'd known,
I'd have gone at it different."

"So you gathered those mangy buffalo tramps—"

"No—Jennisk provided 'em. That's one change I'd have
made. I guess he got 'em because they were cheap. Their
new Henry repeaters came out of the Fort Griffin armory.
Didn't cost him anything. He's the procurement officer there."

"He is a double-dealing crook!" declared Don Ricardo.

"Yeah." Bishop's nod was matter-of-fact. "The point is, you
show up with horses at an Army post and they'll slap you
in the guardhouse! They'll look up your record. It's a
long one, h'm? If a military court didn't send you to the
firing squad, civil law would hang you! So let's talk sense."

"You are doing the talking!" Don Ricardo spoke through
clenched white teeth. "You are leading up to something!"

"What's that smell of scorch? Oh—your clothes. Thought
for a minute it was you burning up." Blandly, Bishop returned to the subject. "I can sell horses to Jennisk, every
head we've got here. He's behind on his quota. With their
papers in order, there's no reason we shouldn't get full
price or close to it. Sixty thousand American dollars, Rico!"

Drawing a quick breath, Don Ricardo tipped up his
gun motioningly at Red. "And this Texan holds the papers
to—"

"Right! We better have him along in case we run into
questions."

"Questions? You said you can sell to Jennisk."

"So I can," Bishop said. "But if we happened to meet a
squad of marshals on the way, or an Army patrol—well,
you and your *ladinos* don't exactly look like respectable horse

traders! Nor me, maybe. Delaney can prove in a minute he's owner of the sorrels. He can vouch for us."

"He had better! And the girl, of course—she will serve the same purpose."

"We're not leaving her here, that's sure!"

Don Ricardo thumb-stroked his singed mustache, eyelids half-lowered, by which Bishop reckoned that he was busily figuring how to play all ends to the middle. An incorrigible trickster, the Don had no intention of sharing the stakes with anybody, least of all Bishop.

"Rogue, have you given thought to how we can get out with the horses?" he inquired, quite willing to pick Bishop's brains and turn the results against him.

"Not yet," Bishop admitted. "It's a tough problem, long as Hump's on our necks. We're way outnumbered."

"How would it be," Red suggested, "if we drove the horses on up the range and kept going? Sera tells me it's flat plains over that way, only water's scarce for a long stretch."

Don Ricardo rejected it. "Our filthy friends down below would soon find out and track after us. They would catch us in open country where those damned rifles would slaughter us!"

"Some of us could stay behind and hold the road."

"Hold the road and watch for cliff-climbers? How many? How long? I have too few men left for that as it is!"

"Still," Bishop said, "we might have to try it. Hump's got supplies to last him, and men enough to come at us in relays 'round the clock, day and night. We're running short of everything but horses. I doubt Sera's got much grub stocked in the house. Not for all of us, anyway." His stomach growled. He thought of last night's supper, and added reminiscently, "She sets a good table."

He watched Don Ricardo pace throughtfully off. He turned

to make a remark to Red, and decided it would be lost on him.

Red, staring hard at him, said, "You're tying in with that bandit for a split in the loot, eh? Birds of a feather! You talked him into a deal—a deal that puts you slap in his class!"

"My talk saved you from a bullet!"

"It saved your hide, too! You couldn't take on his crew if he gave them the nod to blast you down! So you swung over to his side! You sold out to him!"

"I sold him something," Bishop agreed. "It's a fact I can sell the horses, and he can't."

"I lost those sorrels once," Red said, "and I can lose 'em again. But how about Sera's horses? They're part of the loot, and you're ready to earn your share! How about Sera, herself? What becomes of her?"

"The subject," Bishop responded, "has its place in my mind."

"That answer's not good enough!" A taut wildness rang in Red's voice. "I've seen how de Risa looked at her—I've watched his eyes, watched him lick his lips! He's after her!"

Bishop nodded. "So are you. No crime in that. A man wouldn't be human—"

"By God, you're after her, too!"

"What's wrong with that?"

"At your age!" To Red, Bishop—perhaps ten years his senior in years, a hundred in experience—was a holdover from antiquity vaguely connected to the cooling of the earth's crust or thereabouts.

Bishop's eyes chilled, his mouth thinned, and his nose pinched in. Cut to the quick, he rapped, "I'm not so old I can't beat hell out of you at anything you name—fight, drink, cards, or women!"

Somebody then raised a yell that Hump's mob was coming up the pass.

XIII

The buffalo tramps were not staging a creeping attack; they were stamping up the road. They had left their ponies behind and slipped across the river during the cloud-densed darkness. What puzzled Bishop was why Hump had delayed. Some time had gone by since the moon rose clear of the thunderheads. An attack as simple as this one didn't need lengthy planning and preparation.

The narrow pass was a funnel of gunfire, mostly blind shooting in deep shadow. An evening breeze cruised along on schedule and blew into the pass and swept gunsmoke up into the faces of the high-ground men, who sneezed, coughed, cursed, firing blinder than ever.

The attackers stayed hidden below the bends of the steep road, and presently the firing slackened and the air cleared. Bishop found Don Ricardo near him, when he took time out to wipe his eyes and look around. The glance that ran between them was professional, wholly impersonal.

"I'm surprised they tried this a second time today," Bishop said. "Thought they'd take a whack at climbing the cliffs. That'll be next, I guess." He yawned, rubbing his stomach. "I could do with a good meal, a long drink, and a smoke. And some sleep."

"They won't quit, damn them!" Don Ricardo grumbled. "I wish I had more men. If only I had twenty or thirty of my old San Carlos *valientes* here!"

"They were men-and-a-half, all right. I looked for you to come up governor of Chihuahua that time. What went bad?"

"Shot a general. He was a cousin of the *presidente*."

"Tough."

Another puzzle was why Hump's bunch had made so much noise at the start. They were woods-wise, outdoors-wise, and couldn't have forgotten that sound travels upward, especially in a deep and narrow pass. Maybe their minds clung too hungrily to the prize, five hundred remounts, and the dazzling thought left no room for cautious considerations. But they were not pressing the attack. They had hardly showed themselves.

Ten or a dozen men could have made that noise, stamping their feet, then shooting off their Henry repeaters, rapid-fire. Bishop said suddenly to Don Ricardo, "It's a feint!"

"A what?"

"A false alarm—timed to draw us here while the rest climb the cliffs. Take your men and get to it Rico, double pronto! Hell, you should've thought of it! You're losing your edge!"

"*Embustero! Ho, hombres—!*"

The assault up the cliffs was silent until Hump's bark rang out, startlingly near, ordering his mob to the final concerted scramble to the top. They had crept undetected up the clefts and arroyos, while the others made their mock attack on the road, and at the last lap Hump's order brought them swarming, confident that no resistance awaited them on the rim.

It surprised Don Ricardo's men. Half skeptical and nursing some rancor, refusing to run themselves into a sweat, they were fanning out at only a dogtrot. Hump's bark shocked them into a last-minute sprint, but the rim bulged figures before they got to it. They dived to earth, firing their carbines, paying out a prompt surprise on their own account.

While badly outnumbered, they had the advantage of lying prone for steady aim. They made the most of it, and for a minute a blazing battle raged, carbines picking off upcoming targets, Henry repeaters hastily flashing a scattered exchange.

The attackers dropped back. At a shout from Hump they attempted to use the rim as a firing parapet, but the footing was precarious for most of them. They had to expose their heads to the carbines, and when hit they had a long way to fall. More and more of them chose to keep cover, until the rim showed empty.

Red Delaney wiped his face. He spoke to Don Ricardo. "They're climbing back down, hear? Let's go shoot down at 'em!" He started forward. The Mexicans, in favor of it, rose to follow, except three who lay unmoving.

Don Ricardo, reloading his guns and frowning over empty cartridge loops, rapped. "Come back here, hombres!"

They looked at him. "*Por qué?*" asked one.

"You have no shells to waste on the whim of a Texan!"

"We have three dead!"

"So I see. Take their guns and shells, and come with me. Bring the Texan—and knock him down if he tries again to tell you what to do!"

They trooped after him to the road, where they found Bishop seated comfortably chewing on a match in lieu of a cigar. The fact that guarding the pass had turned out to be a soft job, while others banged away for their lives, didn't dent Bishop's conscience.

Don Ricardo had stopped at the house for Sera to join them. "I have lost three more men," he told Bishop, "and we run low on shells. We can't stand them off much longer.

If they make another attack like that one, we're finished. I propose to quit this place right now!"

"Quit where to? On up the range and into the dry country, like Delaney suggested?"

"There's no other way out. We'll have to chance finding water."

Sera, listening, said, "My father didn't find any. He tried once, and had to turn back. The Indians say they know of a few small springs and water holes, but not nearly enough for a band of horses. And they keep the locations secret."

Don Ricardo shrugged. "It's either that, or wait here hoping those scruffy devils won't attack again. I think they will, before the night is over."

"I don't see them pulling out," Bishop agreed, "unless we let 'em have the horses."

"Are you serious? I would kill the horses first!"

"That's about what it would amount to. What horses we didn't lose from thirst, Indians would get. No sense in it. No reason to go off half-cocked into any hellacious badlands."

"No reason?" Don Ricardo echoed. "There are forty or more reasons!"

Bishop nodded. "And you've been too busy with 'em to use your head. Sitting here, I've had time to think. Hump's got to be coaxed into coming full force up this road."

"Coaxed? Full force? We would be—"

"Let two or three of your boys dodge around on the rim, showing themselves. The rest of us will get the horses to milling, making noise for Hump to hear. He's just bright enough to figure we're readying to pull out with the horses, by the dry route, and leaving a small rearguard to cover the cliffs. It ought to bring him up pronto to stop us, by the quickest route—this road! We'll be too busy hand-

124

ling the horses, to make much of a stand, he'll know that."

Don Ricardo blinked. He peered searchingly into Bishop's face. "Have you gone mad? Here we are, short of men and low on shells, and you talk of—*santo sangre!* In a hand-to-hand fight they would slaughter us! We would be wiped out! Man, what are you thinking of? Suicide?"

"No, I'm thinking of how they stampeded two hundred horses at Delaney and me last night and nearly ruined us," said Bishop. "We had to run like hell. I'm thinking it's a fair shake to put Hump on the receiving end tonight. Five hundred spooked horses should do a better job, charging down this pass, h'm?"

He watched Don Ricardo change expression, and went on: "If we time it right—catch 'em when they're halfway up the road, and slam the horses through on a downhill run—it ought to clear the way for us. I doubt they'll take the time to get their ponies before they come up. Hump'll be too anxious, and anyhow those big Henry rifles are unhandy in the saddles. But mounted or afoot, they'll have to scramble fast!"

"And if we can hold our horses bunched—"

"We can outrun their mangy broomtails, once we're clear. Maybe they'll be too damaged to try. With luck, by morning we'll be well on our way up to Fort Griffin."

"Luck has owed me something since you showed up! Of course, this plan of yours would have occurred to me," Don Ricardo asserted, "only—as you said—I have been too busy to think of it. Or a better one."

"Sure." Bishop spat away his chewed matchstick. "Any of you hombres got a good Mexican *cigarro* on you?" One of the men offered a black cheroot. Bishop thanked him and fired it up, grateful for any smoke strong enough to make an impression on his nicotine-pickled palate.

"If and when we get to Fort Griffin with the horses," he

said, "you'll have to lie low, Rico. Stay out of Major Jennisk's sight. I'll do the selling. As for how we'll split the money, we can argue that out later. We don't have it yet."

Don Ricardo shook his head. "Friend Rogue, let us not leave any room for argument between us," he argued, and half-turned away as if pondering on the matter. "I like the plan. That is, up to a certain point. And that point I object to. It is where you speak of selling the horses and then arguing how to split the money. It is too vague, too likely to lead to dispute. I have a more definite proposal to make."

He swung back, his left hand spread out in gesture as a man would when about to offer an explanation. But as he came fully around, a gun glinted in his right hand.

Bishop bit down hard on his cheroot, taken off guard by the unlooked-for maneuver, thinking it ill-timed and senseless. He murmured, "What's this, Rico? What's the idea?"

"No split!" said Don Ricardo. His eyes were brilliantly alert.

"No sale!" said Bishop. He raised his eyes from the gun pointed at him, and was aware that two of the men had grasped Red Delaney's arms. "You'll get nothing!"

Don Ricardo laughed softly. "On the contrary, I get everything! Sixty thousand dollars—"

"Counting your chickens before they're hatched gen'rally makes for disappointment!"

"May I tell you my proposal?"

"Go on!"

"*Gracias!* You will help drive the horses up to Fort Griffin, if we break out of here. Sera and the Texan will sign over to you the bills of sale and whatever other paper nuisance is necessary for you to make the sale to Jennisk."

"That's already settled. And the money? Get to that!"

"You will hand the money over to me, and *I* shall decide about any splitting of it!"

Bishop said reasonably, "It's a long time to hold a gun on me. I'll jump you long before we reach Fort Griffin."

"You won't," Don Ricardo assured him. "I am holding my gun on you only to keep you from drawing on me before I finish explaining my terms. I won't need to, after that."

He allowed the muzzle to droop a little. Bishop dipped a look at it, but made no move, his mind rummaging to what was coming. Sera, staring at them, shifted closer to Red.

"Friend Rogue, you think much of Sera. So does the Texan. So do I. You took long risks for her. So did the Texan. So did I, for that matter. The three of us have—ah —deepest regard for her. May the best man win, eh? I am the best man! I am in command here!"

"For the time being!" Bishop said.

Don Ricardo shook his head. He spoke rapidly, in English, his voice pitched low. "These are my men, remember. They feel that this thing has gone bad. If I tell them we must escape eastward to the dry country, taking the horses, they will ride with me. You and the Texan would stay behind— without horses!"

"You'd set us afoot, h'm?"

"Once, a few years ago, you did that to me! Why shouldn't I return the favor?"

Red, watching the gun, asked, "Does that mean you'd take Sera? On a trip like that?"

"What a question!" Don Ricardo snapped at him impatiently. "Would I leave her here? Abandon her to the mercy of those brutes? Of course I would take her with me! You two would have to put up a fight here, but how long could you last? Long enough to cover our getaway, I hope! I'll gamble I can get through with most of the horses, and sell them to ranchers down the Sabine."

"For thirty dollars a head, no questions asked?"

"Better than nothing. Well, Rogue, what do you want to do?"

"Wring your neck!"

"Naturally, but what is your choice—stay here and die, or take my terms? If it is Fort Griffin, I give you fair warning now that you will not have any chance to try your tricks on me!"

Bishop slanted a look at Sera, at Red. "Fort Griffin it is!" he growled.

And that was his admission that Don Ricardo had him cornered. He stabbed out the cheroot, dourly thinking ahead. It shaped up pretty clearly that a high price was to be paid for having made a flaming fool of Rico, and not all of it in money.

The Don could be lavishly generous at times, but to his mind this thing was a contest between himself and Bishop. Sera was an attractive side-bet. Red Delaney didn't count— a Texan whose title to the sorrels came in useful. The main objective was to beat Bishop, skin him mercilessly, salt him down and rub it in. Pay off all scores.

"All right, Rico, let's get it going."

Don Ricardo's chuckle hit a high note. "You must learn to drop that domineering tone! I shall overlook it this time, but in future remember your position. I am your leader. If you behave yourself I may promote you to my *segundo*." His gleeful chuckling broke off. "First, give up your guns!"

For a moment they stared into each other's eyes. Then Don Ricardo said, a slight break in his voice, "Damn you, Rogue, don't look at me like that! I will shoot, I swear!"

His watching men, conscious of the showdown, raised their carbines. Injured feelings regardless, they would back him up as a matter of course. Bishop remained utterly still, weighing his shrunken chances.

Don Ricardo said more quietly, "I can't let you keep your

guns! In the mix-up, or on the trail, you would—no, I must have them! Now!" he insisted. "Be careful—very careful! If you get off a shot at me, we both go down! Then what? My men will drive the horses east. Sera—how will she end? *Infierno!*" he burst out. "Does your pride blind you? Can't you see I must have your guns?"

At last, slowly, as if under tremendous effort, Bishop spread his coat. He lifted out his pair of guns, butts foremost. He stooped, laid them on the ground, and straightened up, his face a mask.

Red Delaney, his own gun already taken from him, bit his lip and gazed at Sera. Although he was in conflict with Bishop's designs, the gunfighter had stood as a formidable rival to Don Ricardo. With the disarming of Bishop, hopes crashed.

Don Ricardo's sigh of relief was audible. "Arturo Tamargo, come here!" he called. Reaction from tensely strained nerves put a thin lilt into his voice. "Pick up Señor Bishop's guns, Arturo, and take care of them. Take very good care, *sabe?*"

He flashed a grin at Bishop. "And now let us get it going!"

129

XIV

THREE OF THE men scuttled busily about on the rim of the
cliffs, darting and sliding from one spot to another. They set
up a convincing performance that gave the effect of seven or
eight men nervously expecting another attack there at any
minute, and suffering an epidemic of false alarms. By not
shooting at shadows they also gave an indication that ammunition was scarce.

Another man won the job of cat-footing down the pass to
listen for invaders. He took off his boots, for quietness and
speed, and swore by all the saints not to fall asleep down
there.

Don Ricardo and the rest, including Bishop, Red, and Sera,
hurried to the corrals. The first necessity was for everyone
to put a good saddle mount under him, and for several
of them that wasn't simple. They had saddles to spare, but
catching horses for them in the night time was something
else. Moonlight made the roping tricky, and the sorrels did
everything but stand still.

They were, as Red had claimed, fine big horses, full of
spirit, and they had been cooped up too long. They skit-
tered all over the corrals, raising a hullabaloo. Bishop looped
the breeze twice. He could use a rope in everyday style,
but lasso-artistry wasn't essential to poker and powdersmoke.
On his third throw he snared a Mexican.

Sera generously offered him the horse she had caught

and snubbed to the snubbing post in half a minute. Bishop went on roping, so she turned her catch over to Red and dabbed another in quick order. The air was alive with whirling ropes.

Eventually they all got respectably horsed. Then came the task of rounding in the mixed horses from pasture, soothing the disturbed sorrels out of the corrals, and introducing the two bunches together, hoping they wouldn't elect to take off into the wide world easterly.

"Peter's Gates, don't let them run!" exclaimed Don Ricardo as some of the horses skittishly cavorted; and Red muttered back to him, "Give 'em a chance to get acquainted, will you?"

"We don't have much time, after all the noise we've made!"

Red knew horses. So did Sera. They circled leisurely around the two horse herds, crooning nonsense to them, and everbody else drew off and let them work. They knew these horses particularly well—Red the sorrels, Sera the Donavon animals. Maybe knew the language. And their horses knew them.

Mingling, they snuffled one another curiously, raising expectant heads, ears pointed. Red and Sera gently urged them into moving on, still talking gibberish to them. Bishop and Don Ricardo and his riders lined up and closed in, making no abrupt sound or movement. These weren't cattle. These were horses, mettlesome and intelligent, able to dash off and flip their tails farewell if the notion struck them.

The riders eased them on to the yard before the house, there held them bunched, temporarily occupied in striking up snorting acquaintance. The sorrels appeared to have the edge in the social concourse. They formed cliques. Bred of the same strain, they tended to snobbish sniffs at horses of different breeding. Or it may have been because they came

132

from the same range, near Refugio, Bishop thought. Texans down there stuck together.

The barefoot scout came sprinting up the steep road, whispering oaths at sandspurs in his toes. "They come! *Ay* —a hundred, some on ponies! I heard them start up!"

"How many?"

"A hundred at least!"

"A slight exaggeration," commented Don Ricardo. "You must have added in the echoes." Despite his triumphant assumption of leadership, he automatically asked Bishop, "Now?"

Bishop eyed him stonily. "Thought you said you're boss."

"A leader may confer with an underling! Now?"

"Not yet. Let 'em come farther up. Your man was mighty fast on his feet. They're slower."

The seconds dragged by. Beyond the sounds made by the gathered horse herd presently arose a steady, muffled rumbling. It swelled rapidly and separated into padding footsteps, muted clacking of unshod hoofs, hushed voices, creaks and clinks of gear.

The waiting line of riders, listening to the oncoming mob, shifted restlessly in their saddles and sent urgent looks toward Don Ricardo. Their tenseness communicated itself to the quick senses of the horses, causing nervous movement on the fringe of the herd. Don Ricardo opened his mouth to utter the command. Bishop gave himself a measure of dour satisfaction in beating him to it, rasping out a single word:

"*Now!*"

It was a dirty trick on the horses, after wheedling their trust and confidence, and encouraging them in sociably neighboring together—then to squawl suddenly at them like Comanche bucks and lay at them with stinging quirts and rope ends. Two or three of the riders shot off pistols in the air.

Five hundred startled horses jumped. The only way out

lay directly before them, and with one accord they took it. They plunged down into the pass in a ramming, crowding riot. Dust behind them was a choking fog and the roar boomed like a prolonged explosion, as if a massive charge of blasting powder had brought down an avalanche.

When and where they met the upcoming mob could be faintly determined by shreds of yells and some whinnying squeals. Hump and his buffalo tramps had certainly heard the stampede coming at them, but not nearly in time to turn and run before it struck. Here and there one could be dimly glimpsed climbing frantically up the sides of the pass.

The riders hurtled through the boiling ruck of dust, clamped hard in their saddles, their mounts quivering from fear of the wild uproar and of the dark road dropping steeply away beneath racing hoofs. Bishop saw Sera and Red riding together; the sight increased the bleakness of his mood.

He stood to come out loser all around. That Texan, full of protectiveness and kindred emotions, burned to save Sera. If he succeeded, and saved himself as well, she was his. If he didn't—the odds were a hundred to one he couldn't —then Don Ricardo got her and the horses too. A clean sweep.

And, Bishop reflected, the son-of-a-bitch has got my guns.

Don Ricardo swung close across his path at that bad moment, firing a gun—either to help the stampede along, or to stir a climbing buffalo tramp to climb faster.

Bishop shouted savagely at him, "You want me to spill you again?"

Falling back alongside, Don Ricardo called rebukingly to him, "Control your temper, my man! Show a proper respect toward your betters!" He started chuckling at Bishop's glare, but catching sight of Sera with Red, he frowned. "The Texan thinks he is taking care of her, eh? I shall have to—"

"Between them they hold title to all the horses, remember, so you better go easy!"

"Easy? My inclinations—"

"I know your lowdown inclinations! Bottle 'em! Keep your tomcat mind on the horses!"

"Well—until they are sold."

Then they were bursting out of the deep funnel of the pass, wheeling sharply along the strip of beach and gouging gravel; churning across the ford and stringing out to flank the running horses and head them northward. Some ribby Indian ponies slashed leanly into their course, and whirled about in panicked confusion and dashed off.

Behind in the pass, on the road leading up to the empty and abandoned Donavon ranch, a few cursing voices called echoingly back and forth. Somewhere a coyote yapped an insistent summons to its pack.

The herd of horses, requiring much the same kind of handling as a trail herd of cattle, fell into a daily routine after their rattled nerves became more or less calmed down. They covered nearly twenty miles a day on the average, grazing along the way, and were bedded down at night—like cows, except that horses didn't often feel the need to lie down. After midnight they broke off snoozing to graze out a couple of times, moving onward and making another mile or two, which was all to the good.

Around four o'clock in the morning it was get up, saddle up, catch up with the herd. In a wagon outfit the cook would have had some kind of breakfast ready for the crew, if only hot coffee and last night's leftover cold biscuits. The wrangler would have brought up fresh mounts.

But this was a horseback outfit, no wagon, no cook, not a pack or bedroll in the lot. It meant sleeping under saddle blankets, which entailed annoying problems for a tall man when a chilly breeze blew. Some of the Mexicans had woolen ponchos to cover them. They shot somebody's stray steer and roasted the beef in strips wrapped around sticks over a fire. It was a tough old steer, requiring practically all-day chewing to get any good out of it. Hardest on all dispositions was the lack of coffee.

As a lone female journeying and camping with a gang of men, Sera faced particular problems of her own, of a personal nature. Bishop and Red unobtrusively guarded her private retreats, until it became clear that such service was unnecessary. Don Ricardo's mercenary-minded *guerreros* were strictly out for gold.

"We are grown men, not prying boys," Arturo Tamargo remarked to Bishop. Tamargo was the oldest man of the crew, a veteran bandit, and the rest tended to defer to him.

Tough as they were, and coarsely insulting to one another, they could still call up remnants of their native courtesy. They evolved a technique of elaborately ignoring Sera's essential excursions, gazing in an opposite directon while she rode to cover and until she returned. Their general attitude toward her grew indulgent, as if she were a mascot.

At the Jim Ned Creek crossing they met the law.

Although Bishop had mentioned to Don Ricardo that there was some possibility of meeting a squad of marshals or an Army patrol on the trail, privately he hadn't given much weight to it. He had brought it up for the sake of Sera's temporary welfare, and secondarily to save Red Delaney from a bullet. Alive and well, Sera and Red could prove ownership of the horses, if questioned.

A rider on forward scout came racing back, his face solemn. "Five men waiting up ahead!" he sang out. "Lawmen!"

"They spoke to you?" Don Ricardo snapped.

"*Si!* They say we are to halt at the crossing."

The *guerreros* drew their carbines. Don Ricardo looked at Bishop. "You expected this!"

"No, I didn't figure it more'n a chance in fifty. The law's been light around these parts. Five lawmen in a bunch—that's rare."

"What do you make of it?"

Bishop shrugged. "I don't know. Let's halt here and let 'em come to us. It'll give us a little time to get set."

Don Ricardo gave the order, and the riders quickly bunched the horse herd before ranging themselves behind him. He beckoned Red and Sera in, and spoke to them.

"We are about to be questioned by five lawmen. Their lives depend on your answers! If anything goes wrong, we will open fire at once and shoot them down! We will have to—understand?"

"Here they come now," Bishop said. He studied the five approaching horsemen, marking their deliberateness that bespoke a confidence in their authority. "Federal officers, I'd say. Let's hope there are no more behind them."

Don Ricardo swept a glance over his men. They held their carbines before them aslant saddles. Their faces were granite. "Five or fifty, we will not be taken alive!" he stated. That, their answering looks said, went without question.

The oldest of the five reined in a dozen yards from the waiting group, and his four companions lined up with him. He had the bitterly severe countenance of a dyspeptic bigot. His eyes didn't question; they accused. He gave the impression of having complete faith in his ability to judge his fellow men, and the power to bring them to punishment.

For a long minute he inspected the group: Don Ricardo in scorched and split charro finery, a bullet hole through the brim of his sombrero, a gun at each hip; the carbine-armed *guerreros*, some of them wearing bloodstained bandages;

ragged Delaney, Bishop . . . The four younger men gazed gravely at Sera.

From his shirt pocket he took a small gold badge, flashed it briefly, and put it back. "United States marshal. These are deputies." His thin, straight lips barely parted to let his words squeeze out. He picked out Bishop as the head culprit in crime, perhaps because of his attire.

"You got papers on these horses?"

"No," Bishop said. He nodded toward Sera and Red. "They have. They're the owners."

Sera and Red became objects of condemning regard. The marshal snapped his fingers and held out his hand. "Show me!"

"You could take a better tone," Red suggested, nudging his horse forward and digging out his oilskin-wrapped wad of papers. Sera followed him. "My name's Delaney. I'm from Refugio. This is Miss Donavon."

The four deputies raised their eyebrows slightly. Making no reply, the marshal took the wad from Red and opened it, with heavy skepticism. The *guerreros* never moved their eyes from the five.

Don Ricardo whispered to Bishop, "Will those papers get us through?"

"Should—but don't bank on it. Something's in the wind, I don't know what. Look at your men. They're feeling trigger-itchy! Pass 'em a sign to hold back."

Sera and Red watched the marshal frowningly examine their papers. He passed them back reluctantly. "They seem to be in order. Who're these fellows and what are they doing with you?"

"You wouldn't expect Miss Donavon and me to handle five hundred horses on the trail, would you?" Red said. "They're our riders."

"Them? They look like Mexican road agents!"

138

"They're not hired for their looks." Finding himself in the position of defending his and Sera's captors, Red tried to shift off the subject by asking, "What's behind all this?"

He didn't succeed. The marshal stared at Sera. "An unmarried girl in an outfit like this! It—it gags me! It's an abomination!" he declared. "Sinful! Shameless!"

Sera blushed crimson. Like Red, she was not only aligned involuntarily with her captors, but she resented the hectoring attitude of this particular arm of justice. Her eyes flashed. "Is it against the law for me to travel with these men?"

"Against the laws of decency, yes! But it's not our job to enforce those, more's the pity!" He ran a criticizing look over her buckskin pants, which by her shape resembled nothing masculine. "If I was your father—"

"Just what laws are you enforcing?" Bishop interrupted him. "These horses are contracted for delivery at Fort Griffin. You're holding us up."

"Who're you?"

"I'm the agent who's promoting the contract for the parties concerned."

"Oh? A horse dealer, eh?" The marshal scanned him. So did the four deputies, hard. "I'll tell you what laws we're enforcing. The laws against murder and robbery—especially horse stealing! We've been sent out here to check on so-called horse dealers and put a stop to the wholesale stealing of remounts for the Army! We've bagged quite a few already. This looked like our biggest haul so far. I'm far from sure it's not!"

"You've checked the owners' papers."

The marshal waved that aside. "This is a mighty queer outfit. Too much wrong with it! Bound for Fort Griffin, you say, contracted for delivery. Make sure you go there, nowhere else! I'll be keeping close check on you."

139

"Do that. It's where we're going, you'll find."

"And you'll find a difference in Hell's Half Acre. Twenty United States marshals and special deputies are cleaning out the rats' nest. It's finished as the headquarters for cutthroats, outlaws, gunmen—and horse thieves calling themselves horse traders!"

"You get damned personal on short acquaintance!" Bishop observed.

"You don't know how personal I can get! I'm going to look into the recent doings of you and this crew. Where are you from? No, never mind." The marshal nodded stiffly to the deputies, and lifted his reins. "No trouble to backtrack that many horses."

"You're hard to satisfy."

"I'm not satisfied a bit!"

The five lawmen passed the horse herd and rode on down the trail, putting their mounts to a lope. Bishop rubbed his jaw, looking at Sera, at Red, at the *guerreros* fingering their carbines. Don Ricardo expelled a breath.

"I think we should have shot them! They never knew how close they came to dying!"

"Maybe they guessed," Bishop said. "That hidebound old crank's got iron in him, and he's no fool. He couldn't hold us, he knew that. We showed clean papers on the horses, for one thing. All straight and aboveboard. Delivering registered remounts. But we look all wrong to him, Rico! He's certain we're wrong, so he's gone to check back on us."

"We should have shot—"

"Don't kid yourself you and your scrappers could've downed those five without a hell-sight of damage! Federals are tough men to kill! They were on the *cuidado* every second —and me gunless, damn you! And Sera in the middle!"

"But when they get down there, they will find—"

"Plenty, yeah! They won't have to poke around much.

140

Hump's buffalo tramps, dead, damaged, alive. Some of your men, dead. Those Henry rifles, Army issue. Wonder what the marshal will make of it?"

Don Ricardo stared back down the trail, absently stroking the bone handles of his guns. The five lawmen had ridden on out of sight. "He will race us to Fort Griffin and rouse those twenty marshals in Hell's Half Acre!"

"That's about it," Bishop agreed. "He won't try to take us without all the help he can get, and he's not the kind to ask help from any local law between here and Fort Griffin. But we'll have a long start on him. We'll try to stay ahead and get there first. So let's push on—we're wasting time!"

XV

URGED BY THE riders, the horse herd made better time, but it cut down the opportunities for grazing along the way. There was no grain, and the best of horses, lacking feed, couldn't be expected to maintain vigor to keep up the forced pace. Ridden horses flagged and had to be exchanged for fresh ones from the herd, while on the move.

The men, faring no better in the way of nourishment, were gaunt, brittle-tempered. They dropped their bickering insults, for fear of bloody flare-ups. The sense of urgency drove them on. They were racing for a fortune. The fact that a good part of the fortune belonged rightfully to Sera, whom they liked personally, troubled them not at all. Plunder was plunder wherever it came from. Its source was immaterial, impersonal.

"I keep thinking of the twenty marshals at Hell's Half Acre," Don Ricardo said to Bishop. "They will be as suspicious and nosey as that one behind us down the trail— and there may be some among them who know me!"

"I'd make book on that."

"What of yourself? You have kicked holes in the law, too, here and there over the years! I know you are on the blacklists of the Texas Rangers, the Arizona Rangers, the New Mexico—"

"These are United States marshals. They're not hemmed in by state or territorial boundaries. They go in where they're sent or sent for, where it's figured they are needed. When they land on a place like Hell's Half Acre, half the population takes a deep seat in the saddle and a faraway look. They're picked men," Bishop added, enjoying Don Ricardo's increasing uneasiness.

It was a fact, he mused, that in a country not your own you played your cards closer to your chest when all the chips were down. You could be a ringtailed snorter, quite familiar with that country, but you couldn't forget it was alien country and you took extra care. He had experienced it in Mexico.

"Fort Griffin is very dangerous for us, Rogue! Twenty marshals is too many! And the soldiers! I am considering turning off and taking the horses somewhere else to sell."

Bishop shook his head. "It couldn't be long before that marshal found out. I bet he put one of his deputies to moseying somewhere in our rear, keeping check on our course. He's not going to lose track of us as long as we've got the horses! Send a man back to scout, and see if I'm right."

Don Ricardo hailed the order to a *guerrero*, and then repeated Bishop's words. " 'As long as we've got the horses!' Are you trying to talk me into abandoning them—and taking that deep seat in the saddle and a faraway look? Hah! Rogue, you truly *are* a rogue! Can you imagine me doing that? At this stage?"

"You'd have to, if you don't beat the marshal to Fort Griffin! Anywhere else you take the horses, he'll be on your tail with big law!" While he spoke, Bishop let his eyes linger on Sera and Red. They rode together, a short distance off to the side. "No, Rico, you've got to get rid of the horses and scatter, before you shake him off. They're too easy to track. Fort Griffin is your one bet."

"And what of the twenty marshals?"

"You'll have to figure out a way to deliver the horses

without the marshals getting a good look at any of us. Your men won't pass close inspection, any more'n you!"

Bishop turned his eyes back to Sera and Red, wondering what they were finding to talk about. Themselves, probably. They had grown very close together, half the time oblivious to their surroundings and situation. He smothered a sigh, feeling shut out, unwanted.

Maybe, though, they were discussing escape. He scanned their faces. Sera's expression was cool; Red's was troubled. It was about time for that Texan to make his try at a getaway for Sera, if not for himself as well. Fort Griffin wasn't too far off now. A fast run there, a word to those twenty clean-up marshals, and they'd come out on top—five hundred abandoned horses to round up and deliver, cash on the nail. The marshals would help them make delivery, those who weren't busy chasing Rico, his *guerreros*, and a gringo gunfighter without his guns.

"No," Sera said, "I can't believe he's as bad as you think he is."

"He's out for himself all the way!" declared Red. "There's no real difference between him and de Risa! They're old sidekicks who've ridden outlaw trails together!"

"Sidekicks? De Risa forced him to take terms and give up his guns!"

"I gather they don't hit it off when there's money in sight. Bishop would've done the same to de Risa, given the chance. I've seen him operate. He's hard as they come."

"I've seen a sort of kindly side to him."

"Oh, I grant he's human—"

"That's very generous of you!"

"Human enough," Red finished his sentence, "to show a kindly side to a girl he finds attractive! He as good as told me he's after you."

"I take that as a compliment," Sera responded contrarily, her face warming. "And I don't forget he saved my life."

"I guess he saved mine, too—mostly because I'd be useful when it came to proving ownership of the sorrels! That was when he was still hoping somehow to beat de Risa and grab everything for himself." It was difficult for Red to give credit to a rival. "Now that he's lost out all around, he'll try to save his own skin!" An unbidden imp of jealousy stung him, and he ended, "Bishop's pulled the wool over your eyes, like de Risa did!"

Sera's color heightened. Perversely, she twisted his meaning. "Are you sure he's lost out all around? I don't believe he saved my life because I own horses. He saved me from de Risa, too, and that's another debt of gratitude I owe him. If he saves me again, from this"—she took a breath to steady her voice—"I don't think he will have lost out *all* around!"

In contrast to her deep flush, Red's face whitened around the mouth. For a while he couldn't speak; then he said strainedly, "I'm sorry I brought that on. It must have cost you a lot to say it."

At once remorseful, her eyes glistened wet. "It did—to say it to you, Red. Forgive me."

"I won't say another word against Bishop, except one thing. Whether you believe it or not, he and de Risa are two of a kind and if Bishop had won we'd be no better off— because they both aimed for the same thing!"

"I'm not convinced, but I can't change your mind."

"No. We've got to get ourselves out of this, Sera, and we don't have much time left. In a couple of days we'll reach Fort Griffin. If nothing stops them they'll sell the horses. De Risa gets the money. I don't know what he figures on doing with Bishop, or with me. But you—"

"I've had nightmares, Red!"

146

"So have I!"

Their eyes locked. Sera started a reaching movement toward him. She let her arm fall, glancing swiftly around. "Can we escape?"

"We've got to! Maybe we can make it to Fort Griffin ahead of them—warn the commander, tip off the marshals at Hell's Half Acre. We'll make the break together. It's got to be timed right, so watch for me to give you the sign. Here's how we'll work it . . ."

Those two, Bishop conjectured, had plotted a getaway. He hoped Don Ricardo hadn't been watching them closely. Their faces betrayed them. They weren't equipped with the long-learned craft and guile to mask a desperate resolve. No lessons in double-dealing, and small talent for it. Red Delaney's expression was stern, tense, and at the same time furtive. Sera looked almost guilty. Bishop caught her eyes and sent her a grave nod.

Don Ricardo rode up from behind and said to him, "You were right. The man I sent back tells me one of the deputies is trailing after us, well in the rear."

"So you better keep on to Fort Griffin."

"It annoys me to be followed. A couple of my men could drop back and take care of that one!"

Bishop shook his head. "He'll be way too cagey to fall for a 'buscado. Bet he's swinging wide past any spot that looks like it might hide a carbine or two. If you tried for him and missed, where would you be?"

"No worse off, as I see it!"

"I see it different. The deputy would carry the word that you tried to bushwhack him. We'd have every federal man in the country on our necks!"

"We will have that in any case! By this time that iron

147

marshal has found what we did to Hump and his buffalo tramps."

"Sure. But we're a jump ahead of him. Let's keep it that way. He'll have poked around there for a while, reading sign, putting two-and-two together before starting up after us."

Don Ricardo eyed Bishop narrowly. "I feel that you are hiding something up your sleeve! Twenty federal men at Hell's Half Acre, a deputy at our rear, the marshal racing us to Fort Griffin to set a trap for us—yet you insist on—"

"I'm saying it's too late now to turn off this trail. The deputy behind us would ride on and report it. He's got his orders, you can depend on it." Bishop's eyes strayed fleetingly to Sera and Red; they had parted. "If Fort Griffin's a trap I'm in it, too—and without a gun!"

"That you certainly are!" Don Ricardo agreed. "At the right time I will tell you when to ride on alone and find out if there is a trap set for us! Nobody is better fitted for the task than you, my good segundo!"

"Unarmed?"

"If the federal men are as tough as you say they are, your guns would not stand off twenty of them! No, your task will be to scout for any trap, right up to the fort itself."

"You mean spring it for you, so you'll have a warning to make a getaway!"

"That is logical, no?"

Sera reined her horse off the trail, toward thick brush lying to the right, and those of the *guerreros* who noticed her withdrawal followed their adopted custom of turning their eyes away. It had become a common routine.

The day was waning. Soon the tired and underfed men would throw the horse herd off the trail and make meager camp for the night. They had met no luck at finding another

stray cow, and on Don Ricardo's orders the outfit had by-
passed the few small towns and roadhouses along the way.
Don Ricardo was taking no chances on the temptations of
delays, of drink and unguarded talk, listening ears, inquisitive eyes. He tongue-lashed a rider for attempting to slip
back to a roadhouse, and threatened to shoot the next one.
His temper was fraying, like theirs, strained between the
punishing present and the toss-up of the near future.

Bishop watched Red Delaney casually advance his position along the right flank of the driven horse herd, until he
was close up front. Red, he noted, had changed to a fresh
horse. So had Sera. This, then, was the minute.

"Rico, he inquired, "where did you get that rifle in your
saddle boot?"

"From the Donavon ranch," Don Ricardo answered shortly, preoccupied with the problems and hazards of turning
five hundred hard-won horses into gold.

"Looks like a Whitneyville .69 to me."

"No, Remington .58 is what it is."

"Let's see it."

Don Ricardo slid him an ironic stare. He drew the rifle
from the saddle boot, carefully unloaded it, and held it
out. Bishop took it from him.

"You're right, it's a Remington." He went on scrutiniz-
ing it. "Model 1863. You don't see many of these. Made in
Connecticut, like the Whitneyville. Always made 'em big
caliber, those New Englanders, for the Union Army. Knock
a man flat at a pretty fair range, this thing."

Don Ricardo nodded. "I could. A big man, easily. About,
say, your size!"

"That's an unfriendly thought, Rico!"

A sudden commotion up ahead broke off their sharpen-
ing discussion. Men raised yells of warning. A gunshot exploded, causing horses along the right flank of the herd to

shy, and then a hasty hammering of carbines brought the whole herd into rearing disorder.

Two riders—Sera and Red—were streaking off together away from the trail. Bent low on their stretched-out horses, they veered fast from one patch of covering brush to another. Sera had started first from her visit into the thick brush, and Red, on cue, had cut out after her. He rode close behind, to shelter her as best he could from the carbines.

Within seconds, Red's sheltering maneuver grew unnecessary. The carbines, short-barrel saddleguns lethally accurate within their limits, were not designed for long-range shooting. Falling short, bullets kicked spurts of earth behind the escaping pair. Arturo Tamargo led three *guerreros* in pursuit after them, but their mounts weren't as fresh as those that Sera and Red had foresightedly provided for themselves.

"The rifle—give me!" Don Ricardo reached out to Bishop for the unloaded Remington .58.

Bishop, making to pass it over to him, clumsily let its butt smack the horn of his saddle. The rifle tipped over, batted Don Ricardo on his sombrero, and fell to the ground. "Wup—sorry!"

Don Ricardo jumped off his horse, swearing in Spanish. Bishop also dismounted, and both bent down at the same time to retrieve the dropped rifle. Their heads met and the sombrero took another crusher. Don Ricardo's swearing gained lurid force.

Picking himself up and freeing his crumpled ears from the jamming sombrero, he snarled at the nearest man, "Hold Bishop off!"

The man slung up his carbine, its muzzle aimed at Bishop's face. Bishop said moderately, "Now, Rico, don't get so riled over a little accident."

"Stay clear of me, damn you!"

150

Snatching up the rifle, Don Ricardo rammed in the single heavy cartridge. He sank to one knee, butt to his shoulder, holding the Remington steady. His eyes, hot black, searched for the two fugitives.

The time wasted had allowed Sera and Red to gain a good distance. Enough, Bishop thought, for them to make good their getaway, provided misfortune didn't trip them. They had put so much brush behind them now that only an occasional glimpse of them could be seen. Even Rico, crackshot that he was, could easily miss a flitting target at that distance, having to gauge in an instant the trajectory and lead. He wouldn't have time to reload. And maybe, just maybe, the Remington was faulty.

The two riders emerged into sight, flashing across a bare expanse of ground that would take them around a ridge and safe off yonderly. Arturo Tamargo and the three *guerreros* with him had a hopeless chase.

The Remington roared its single discharge.

For a second or two Bishop believed Don Ricardo had missed. He was watching intently for a spurt of earth, when Red Delaney and his horse crashed a fearful cropper. He let out his breath and transferred his watching to Sera.

She looked back. She rode on a short way, sawing reins, her horse jolting, slowing, then turning about to gallop to Red, halting by him. She slipped out of her saddle, bent over Red, tried to help him up.

Arturo Tamargo and the three *guerreros* rode into the bare expanse. They ranged themselves swiftly around Sera, surrounding her, cutting off escape, and closed in.

Don Ricardo crackled orders to throw the horse herd off the trail and make camp before darkness set in. Finished with that, he confronted Bishop.

"So you knew they had plotted an escape together! You knew to the minute when they would make a break! You

151

tried to help them, tried to keep me from using the rifle Why? They would have ridden straight up to Hell's Half Acre and set those twenty federal lawmen onto us!"

He waited for a reply from Bishop. None came. He said tightly, "They nearly got away! I shall take no more risks on having that happen again. They will be treated as prisoners—as prisoners should be treated! And you, too!"

Thinking his own thoughts, only half hearing the bitter words spoken to him, Bishop nodded absently. In the gathering dusk he saw Arturo Tamargo returning with Sera and Red—Red riding double behind Tamargo, hanging on to him. That banged-up horse breeder. That busted Texan.

She had turned back for him. With escape for herself practically a sure thing; with safe cover only a few lengths away, and a good fresh horse under her—she had turned back for him. Tried to pick him up. Wouldn't quit him.

"Rico," Bishop said at last, "we're both goddam fools!"

Taken aback, Don Ricardo asked, "How is that?"

"We each had our chance once to win what we wanted, but we waited to win more. That's where we missed out."

Don Ricardo stared peculiarly at him as if he had lost his mind. "Do you forget that everything is in my hands?"

"Everything was in *my* hands, for a while back there."

"The past is past!"

"And the future isn't here yet."

XVI

THEY LAY TIREDLY around a fire that they had lighted from sheer habit and were allowing to die because tonight there was nothing left to cook. Spirits sank to low ebb in the hungry camp as the night wore on and a north wind moaned through.

Don Ricardo, himself not immune to the edgy mood of depression, sat up to deliver a scathing lecture on ingratitude and bad faith. The fact that he, as a faithless highbinder, took a cynical view of gratitude, did not handicap him. He was wound-up like a steel spring to the last notch.

"You were given a privilege and you abused it!" he let go at Sera. "I let you have a large amount of freedom, allowed you to ride your pick of the horses, placed no guard over you—and you betrayed my trust!"

He had given the order that henceforth she and Red were to be kept strictly separated. Not a word or sign was to pass between them. His anger was directed chiefly at Sera, and Bishop understood why. Don Ricardo fancied himself as a lady-killer, with sufficient reason—he could usually win any woman he went after, by one means or another. If the winning entailed a judicious use of drugged wine, he regarded it as merely an aid to his masculine charm, releasing the fair one from her troublesome restrictions of modesty.

In attempting to escape from him, with another man, Sera

153

had wounded his vanity. Gallant flourishes and burning glances, calculated to stir upheavals in the maidenly breast, had gone begging. She found him less than irresistable. She actually let her preference lean to a shabby damned Texan. It was humiliating, insulting.

His violence-studded way of life had not coarsened him to the point, as yet, where he might offer outright brutality to a young and pretty female who had captured his susceptible passions. He had to search for ways to punish her. In reaching for strong censure his speech grew somewhat stilted and highflown.

"You have taken advantage of my indulgence!" he charged Sera. A man yawned loudly. Don Ricardo's nostrils thinned. "You make it necessary to place close guard over you. Arturo Tamargo, see to it that she is never allowed out of sight! Not for a minute, not one second, is she to—"

"Oh, come off it, Rico!" Bishop growled. He sat by Sera, keeping her company. She had no trepidations about any of the *guerreros* taking personal liberties with her, but she seemed to draw some comfort from having Bishop beside her. He felt her huddle closer to him, beginning to tremble under Don Ricardo's wrath, like a guilty child denounced by a schoolmaster.

"What?" Don Ricardo stabbed a look at him. He rose to his feet. "You and the Texan, too, are under close guard! You are not to get out of sight, understand?"

Bishop shrugged. "That's about the way it's been since we left the Donavon ranch. Not Sera, though. That's different."

"She brought it on herself!"

"I said it's different with her. It stays different."

"I give all orders here," Don Ricardo began, "and—"

"You puffed-up son of a buzzard!" Bishop flared at him. "A young lady's got a right to privacy once in a while, if there's any around. Do I have to tell you reasons? Where the hell were you drug up—in a goat yard?"

The question stung Don Ricardo's face red, he having always claimed to be by birth a blueblooded hidalgo descended from Spanish conquistadores, gentlemen-in-arms trailing long strings of titles. He sat down. "Er, um, she"—he swallowed—"she will take her privacy on foot, by my order. As for you—"

"S-ss't!" Arturo Tamargo lifted a hand. "Listen!"

They fell silent, holding their breaths, listening. The horse herd was quiet, but the north wind rustled the brush. A steady cadence of hoofbeats, muffled by distance, made itself heard. Somewhere a single horseman rode at a lope in the darkness.

"The deputy! Riding north!" Don Ricardo's murmur was flat. "Riding to warn the federal lawmen! Why now? What could he have found out, back there behind us?"

"He must've heard the shooting, sundown," Bishop said.

"Ah, yes. Perhaps he saw something of what happened, too. Enough to send him on to report."

The beat of the loping horse died out. Some of the men had risen. They lowered themselves back to the earth, shaking their heads briefly. No catching that fast rider in the dark; he could outdodge any pursuit.

Don Ricardo slid a dead glance at Sera. "You and your Texan made good on half your purpose. You did not get away—but you have put the law onto us." He took his eyes off her to stare into the fire for a long minute. In a gesture of resignation he slapped his thighs and stood up. "We're finished!"

Bishop scanned him, trying to read his mind, speculating as to his intentions and preparing his own countermoves in advance. He concluded that Rico was ready to throw in his hand and get out, grabbing whatever he could. That intention had to be scotched. He couldn't see Sera as salvage. She'd do to take along, but not by Rico.

"You giving up?" he asked him, and got a crooked smile.

"Why go on? If we don't meet the federal men somewhere up the trail tomorrow, they will be waiting for us at Fort Griffin! That deputy will get there in the morning, given a change of horses along the way. I feel a homesickness for Mexico!"

"And let these horses go, eh?"

Don Ricardo nodded. "It is sad to abandon the herd," he sighed, "but it is marked, too easily traced, and can't travel as fast and far as I wish. My men and I will take the pick of them for our needs, of course. Then it's— How do you say?— A deep seat in the saddle and a faraway look, yes!"

"And Sera."

"And Sera."

"It's a big loss you're taking," Bishop said, his tone dispassionate. "Sixty thousand dollars, tossed over your shoulder, this close to Fort Griffin."

"Too close!" said Don Ricardo. "Fort Griffin is a death-trap now, not a market for the horses. And it is too late to try selling them somewhere else. A big loss, yes. I regret it." He spread his hands. "I have lost fortunes before. There will be compensations. I shall console myself."

"Sera."

"Sera."

The *guerreros* had not been wholly following the drift, and Don Ricardo began explaining to them logically the reasons that compelled his decision to slant for Mexico. He worked up toward it gradually, careful to remove any blame from himself, knowing the ready tempers of his men.

Bishop broke in. He spoke slowly, bluntly, deepening his tone to a harsh growl.

156

"Your high and mighty Don Ricardo de Risa is about to throw away sixty thousand dollars in horses—for a woman! Yes, this one, this girl, Sera. Is she worth it? Maybe she is to a tomcatting *mico* like him, but how about you? Hell, they're partly your horses!"

His words brought them lunging erect, while Don Ricardo stepped back in dismay, shaking his head at them and waving his hands in a vain effort to quell their uproar. Bishop, having touched off the blaze, waited to fan the flames.

"What?" bellowed Arturo Tamargo, taking the lead as spokesman for all. "After our hard work and trouble? Our fighting? Our victory over the Hump *animaluchos?* Our dead? Our wounds? Our aching muscles and growling guts?" He shook his carbine high in the air. "Give up the horses now? No! By the blood of all the saints—no, no, no!"

"No!" they thundered.

"Sooner would we shoot the girl!" Arturo Tamargo vowed, prodding his carbine toward Sera. "*Ay,* and certain others!" he added meaningfully.

"You liar!" Don Ricardo snarled at Bishop. He held a gun cocked at him. "You madman!" He spoke to the *guerreros.* "It is not for the girl that I would give up the horses! Bishop lies to you!"

"Then what is your reason?" demanded Arturo Tamargo. "The lawmen?"

"Yes, the lawmen! That deputy who passed tonight is on his way to Fort Griffin—to Hell's Half Acre where there are twenty federal lawmen! You must know what that means!"

The *guerreros,* reconsidering, began cooling off. The clamor subsided to mutterings.

"The federal lawmen will either set out to meet us on the trail," Don Ricardo continued, "or they will trap us at Fort Griffin." He wiped his face with his hand, giving them a mo-

157

ment for further reconsidering. "Fort Griffin is out. What can we do? Take the horses elsewhere to sell? No. Those lawmen will be fast on our heels. Take what horses we need and head home to Mexico? Yes! And soon, or we will never get out of this cursed country alive! I tell you the truth, *amigos!*"

Some of them nodded reluctantly. Others heaved heavy sighs, hating the thought of giving up rich plunder. Arturo Tamargo pulled gloomily at his lower lip. "It goes against one's principles," he grumbled. "*Qué desgracia*—such a waste!"

It was time to fan up the waning flames. "Do we know for sure it was the deputy who rode by?" Bishop queried. He saw Red Delaney watching him critically. "No, we don't," he answered his own question before somebody challenged it. "None of us got a look at him. Could've been anybody."

"Pah!" Don Ricardo snorted. "One doesn't have to see the coyote to know its howl."

"How did a coyote get into this? Let's keep to the subject, Rico. You're howling before you're hurt!"

The barb brought appreciative grins from the listeners, whose native wit leaned toward subtle insult carved from an opponent's own words. Don Ricardo's eyes flickered dangerously.

"Allowing it was the deputy," Bishop said, "what had he got on us? He heard some shots. Maybe he saw Sera and the Texan try to scoot off. All right, so he reports it. Do you think, on the strength of that, twenty federal officers are going to drop everything and come at us? It was a private affair. Nobody got killed."

He was getting his argument across, patching it up as he went, convincing them without convincing himself. Their faces showed a returning of indignation, and of encouragement. They were only too willing to believe that their venture was not a failure. His pseudo-optimism was vastly more palatable to them than Don Ricardo's realistic pessimism.

"Your reasoning," Don Ricardo countered acidly, "is completely false, and you know it! The 'private affair' is not all that the deputy will report. It is one more nail in the coffin! The old marshal—"

"He's the one with the goods on us, I grant that. He's found evidence enough against us, below the Donavon ranch, to curl his hair! He might even have caught Hump alive, for all we know. But he's behind us. He hasn't caught up with us yet."

The *guerreros* nodded vigorously to that. A plain fact, nothing truer. Don Ricardo slapped his leg in exasperation. "That deputy got his orders from the marshal to—" he began, and again Bishop interrupted him.

"A deputy's only a deputy. He can't go ordering all those U.S. marshals around. Anyhow, Sera and Delaney still hold clear title to the horses. We're still driving for 'em—bound for Fort Griffin where we make delivery and collect the cash! Eh, hombres?"

The hombres voiced hearty approval, voting him a man of clear vision and foresight, not to be misdirected from the main objective by petty details and trifling obstacles.

"Nothing's changed," Bishop ended, which he himself thought was a pretty sweeping statement, very thinly justified. He brushed past Don Ricardo's drawn gun, walked over to Red, and gazed impassively at him.

"What game are you playing?" Red whispered.

Bishop scratched the back of his neck. "Damned if I know!" he admitted. "Playing for time, I guess. You want Rico to take Sera down on a Mexican honeymoon?"

"God, no!"

"Nor me. So play along. Rico's got to go along with his

159

men now. He could kill me for crossing him, but he can't go against his whole crew."

"What's going to happen at Fort Griffin?" Red asked.

"Your guess is as good as mine," Bishop said. "We might not get there. Rico's right—the deputy's going to stir up those marshals. They're hungry for horse thieves. The least they'll want to do is hold us for investigation."

"And that'd give the old marshal time to get in his licks. But I reckon these hombres wouldn't be took!"

"It'd be tough." Bishop fingered his empty holsters. "That's not your worry."

"No. How's Sera? They won't let me near her."

"She's all right."

They were silent, until Red said quietly, "You still hope somehow to beat de Risa, don't you? He's got your guns. He's got you like a—like a caged tiger. And you're watching every minute to get a claw into him!"

Bishop quirked an eyebrow, faintly amused. "I'm looking for openers."

Red met his eyes. "I hope you don't make it. The best thing that can happen for Sera and me is for this outfit to run up against the United States marshals. If you managed by some miracle to beat de Risa, it'd be bad for us. I know the kind of tiger you are. You'd find a way to sell the horses. We'd be no better off than we are now. Not me—nor Sera! Especially Sera!"

"Matter of opinion," Bishop said, and walked away.

Don Ricardo stalked up to him, his face furious, dark eyes snapping. Among all the fantastic scrapes that he had got in and out of during the course of his gaudy career, never had he been forced to contend with open mutiny. He prided himself upon being a born leader.

"Your deceiving tongue is sending this outfit into almost

certain disaster!" he accused Bishop bitterly. "I have a mind to take Sera and pull out!"

Bishop shook his head. "The crew won't stand for it. They know she's needed, like Delaney, to prove title to the horses. Try it and see! You could pull out by yourself. No objections there."

"And leave everything to you!"

"Sure. I'll either collect or—"

"What odds would you give on collecting?"

"Damn short, but I'm laying my neck on the line. Too much of a gamble for you, Rico? Well, a man can't keep his nerve up all the time. I've seen the best of 'em crack. Remember Buckskin Frank?"

"My nerve is as good as ever," retorted Don Ricardo, "but I am not crazy! Fort Griffin—it is as madbrained as riding into a camp of Texas Rangers!"

"Then why don't you tuck your tail under and run? Maybe I'll get to look you up someday in Mexico. Buy you a drink."

Eying Bishop venomously, Don Ricardo said, "No, I am staying in charge. But you will ride forward, heading the outfit. You should, as it is your doing that we go on to Fort Griffin! You talked yourself into that job!"

"Guess I did," Bishop allowed. "Where'll you be while I'm riding up front?"

"With Sera at the rear, watching you!"

"Better give me my guns."

"Guns? I wouldn't trust you with a slingshot, Rogue!"

"H'm!" Bishop got a mental picture of himself riding ahead of the outfit, unarmed, scouting for lawmen and other hazards from here to Fort Griffin. "If and when the marshals come at us—" he began.

"Talk them out of it!" crooned Don Ricardo with malicious pleasure. "Talk them out of it!"

XVII

A RIDER TOPPED a nearby hill and halted there to survey the outfit of Mexicans driving the horse herd up the trail. He wore a badge pinned openly to his shirt; it glinted in the sun. Bishop raised his head and laid a deliberate stare at him. The man paid back the stare, scanning him thoroughly. He reined his horse around smartly and dropped out of sight.

That made the third. They're keeping close check on us, Bishop mused, and they want us to know it.

Don Ricardo cantered up from the rear and pulled in alongside. "What do you make of it, Rogue?" he inquired blandly. "They seem to show special interest in you! Perhaps it is only because here in front you are so conspicuous, eh?"

"They're making sure we're the outfit they've been told to expect," Bishop said. "I'm part of the description."

"We are not disappointing them. Stay in your conspicuous position, please! It is becoming hard on your nerves? You look anything but cheerful!" Grinning, the Don rode back.

He, contrarily, grew more recklessly cheerful with each mile, his spirit of daring fully alive. Bishop had forced his hand, but he in turn had thrown the play back to Bishop and placed him where he could do no mischief. Bishop had found nothing yet in the way of openers, and the prospects didn't promise any.

Don Ricardo rode jauntily, his damaged sombrero cocked

at a dashing slant. Whenever he caught sight of Bishop's bleak visage he chuckled. "There goes the man who will make me a fortune, or ride into the guns of the marshals!" he commented to Sera. "And it is by his own choice. If he is lucky, I win!"

"And if he is unlucky?"

"Then by his bad luck we will have warning in time to get away. As for the horses"—he shrugged—"I already resigned myself to losing them."

"My horses," Sera said, "and Red's."

His glowing gaze caressed her. "I shall give you other riches, *vida mia!*"

"*Vida mia,*" she echoed. "That means 'my life,' doesn't it?"

"Yes. You are my life."

"Perhaps I shall be your death!"

He laughed lightly as if she had voiced a harmless quip. His attitude toward her was that of a knight to a captive princess: scrupulously courteous—and possessive. By means of elegant manners he rose superior to his scorched and split garb.

On the bank of Clear Fork he called a halt. Irritatingly cheerful, he remarked to Bishop, "I am surprised that the marshals have not swooped down on you! Congratulations!"

"We've got about two miles more to go yet," Bishop said. He half-wished that he hadn't talked so convincingly to Don Ricardo's *guerreros*. Riding in the forefront, every minute expecting a squad of federal law officers to confront him, strained his nerves. "They can still jump us."

"If they were going to, they would have done it before now," Don Ricardo disagreed. "Their spies know where we are and where we are going. I think it most likely they are waiting for us at Fort Griffin. So," he said pleasantly, "we will go no farther until we find out."

Bishop eyed him. "Meaning?"

"Meaning you, friend Rogue! You will ride on to the fort, to discuss horses with Major Jennisk. Sera and the Texan will first sign those confounded papers over to you, making you the owner. You can show them to the marshals—if they give you the chance!"

"It's me they'll look at, not any papers!"

Don Ricardo flashed his white-toothed grin. "With your gifted tongue, perhaps you can persuade them into letting you sell the horses to Major Jennisk. If you perform that miracle, then get the major to send some soldiers out to meet the horse herd and take it in. I am shy about entering the fort. So are my men."

"I don't look forward to it, either!" said Bishop.

"If the marshals pounce on you—well, I shall miss you, Rogue! But you dug your own pitfall, no?"

"S'pose I tell you to go to hell?"

For reply, Don Ricardo spoke to his *guerreros*. "Señor Bishop might be able to sell the horses. Nobody else could do it for us. I am sure he will not refuse to try!"

Their looks said Bishop had a short life ahead of him if he did refuse.

"I am going with him, to keep his mind on his task," Don Ricardo continued. "Arturo Tamargo, start drifting the horses on up the trail after we leave. If you see soldiers coming down to meet you, drop back and let them take over. Return here and wait. Keep close guard over the young lady and the Texan!"

"Soldiers?" muttered Tamargo. "Soldiers?"

"Cavalrymen, yes. But if you see lawmen coming instead, then run for it! The chances are you will see *me* coming—fast! In either case, don't leave the Texan alive, and don't leave the young lady behind! Well, Rogue?"

"How about my guns?" Bishop asked.

Don Ricardo shook his head. "Sorry, the answer is still

'no!' I will not take that chance with you." He pulled out the heavy Remington .58 rifle from its saddle boot and held it resting across his saddle. "I am riding behind you to see you enter the fort. I shall be waiting within rifleshot for you to come out. If you pull off your miracle and sell the horses, you might take a fancy that the money is yours! My rifle will relieve you of the temptation to run off with it!"

He intercepted Bishop's glance at Sera, and he smiled and said, "She may be a guarantee that you will come back here if you can. A hostage, to insure your good behavior. But as you yourself asked—is she worth giving up sixty thousand dollars for? My rifle is a guarantee that I can depend on!"

Without replying, Bishop swung aboard his horse and set off for Fort Griffin, Don Ricardo following him at fifty yards' distance. There was nothing else for it, and he broodingly reflected that Rico had him about cooked. From the first, this thing had gone wrong.

Partly because of his gunless state, Bishop turned off the trail before it took him through Hell's Half Acre. His black coat, by its severely respectable length, cloaked his empty holsters, but there were men who possessed a kind of instinct about such conditions and could sense whether you were armed or not. Also, he didn't propose to make matters easier for the vigilant marshals.

Skirting around the town, he circled over toward Fort Griffin on its hill. The remembered sounds of the town were absent; when he had left they could be heard a mile off— the thumping pianos, barkers bawling the merits of gambling dens, drunks singing, trail hands turning loose the curly wolf. The big law had moved in and tamed Hell's Half Acre.

"Town's dead," he muttered, not without a tinge of regret. Although there hadn't been much that was good about

166

the place, it did have a wild individuality, one that challenged a man to stretch his brains.

Even the fort wore a humdrum aspect, as if infected by the dull affliction. Outside the rear stockade, washing strung on clotheslines struck a domestic note, and smoke from chimneys told of evening meals in preparation. They had their married quarters, their commissary and sutler's store; the fort was self-contained to some degree. Hell's Half Acre had probably been placed off-limits to the garrison, by request of the clean-up marshals, until they got the town scrubbed down to a pale shadow of piddling propriety. The law was all very well, but too much of it was apt to blight natural growth and independent spirit.

Bishop rode aslant up the hill, angling toward the fort's open gates from which the road ran down to the town. Don Ricardo, stopping at the bottom, sent a whistle up after him and motioned backward. Bishop looked, and counted seven men.

They had come out to the edge of the town, to stand gazing after him, wearing their badges, their guns, purposely giving him notice that they had him marked. If Don Ricardo held any special interest for them, they didn't show it. The center of attention was Bishop, and he could feel the weight of their absorbed regard.

He looked again at the gates of the fort. A sentry on duty there, watching him, turned his head and spoke to someone. For Bishop, the fort then lost its humdrum aspect. He called down to Don Ricardo, "Where'll you be?"

Don Ricardo pointed to a lone giant oak farther along the foot of the hill. "Taking my ease in the shade! Good luck!"

Shade, Bishop thought. Not much shading left, the sun going down. The value of the oak was that it stood well within rifle-shot of the gates. Rico could hold the drop on him going and coming, with the Remington .58. He rode on up to the gates and was about to make known his business to the sentry, when a cold-eyed lieutenant stepped out.

"Dismount," said the lieutenant quietly. Bishop got down off his horse. The lieutenant stepped behind him. "I must search you for firearms. Orders." He touched the empty holsters, made no comment, then patted Bishop's armpits and waistband.

"Proceed, Mr. Bishop. The major's expecting you."

Bishop said, "I bet!" He led his horse on in, ignoring the lieutenant's directions.

He had never been actually inside Fort Griffin before, as Major Jennisk had been careful to conduct their conversation in the privacy of the outdoors while they walked up the road from the town. Wanting to discover what he was getting into, Bishop rounded a corner of the armory and continued on, passing by the adjutant's office. He came to the central parade ground and paused to get his bearings: officers' quarters, barracks, stables, a double row of tiny houses crowding a rear corner.

A bugle sounded a fast, triple-tongue summons, bringing an orderly rush of men to the stables. A voice sang out in bored mockery to the tune of the call:

"Oh, go to the stable, all you who are able,
And give your poor horse some hay and some corn!"

Another trooper took up the chant:

"For if you don't do it, the Captain will know it,
And you will catch hell as sure as you're born!"

Nothing out of line here. No break in the measured routine of the day. Bishop listened to the busy sounds coming from the stables. If anything was amiss—if the law had prepared a reception for him—the troopers would at least have got rumor of it. Their commonplace behavior denied that they had any inkling of anything unusual.

And yet, those seven federal lawmen, watching him ride here to the fort . . . The scouting deputies along the trail. The deputy who had raced on ahead.

Unsatisfied, he cut on across the parade ground, now empty. A hurrying captain emerged from officers' quarters, paid him a preoccupied nod, and hurried on. Bishop didn't try to detain him. What he sought was an enlisted man, preferably a noncom, to exchange words with and observe his reactions. A noncom would have a close idea of what was going on; they knew everything worth a bit of gossip around an Army post.

He turned into the narrow street between the double line of tiny houses, and guessed this was Soapsuds Row. He knew it for a fact when a huge hamper of washing came rocking up the street, borne in the clasp of two brawny red arms. His horse promptly shied and reared at what, to it, was a frightening monstrosity. He hauled it down, stamping and snorting.

"Stop yer horse from raisin' dust all over me nice clean washin'!" a woman bellowed. She poked her face around the hamper in her arms. "A civilian! Who d'ye think y'are an' what're ye doin' here? No visitors 'thout p'mission! Git out!"

She was Irish, and Army from way back. Being on Soapsuds Row, she had to be the wife of a sergeant, privileged to take in laundry for pay. She probably knew the drill manual backward.

Bishop doffed his broad-brimmed hat to her. He bowed gravely, masking his saturnine mood. "Forgive me, miss! I have an interview due with Major Jennisk, and losing my way like a fool in luck I blunder into the path of sweet femininity! I'm not regrettin' me error, for at its worst—which is grand—I have seen the fair face of a lady! Allow me the pleasure to carry your burden to your door."

The broad, sunburned face of the large woman softened. "Yer talk don't humbug me, but the words are nice," she sighed, and set down the hamper. "Ye big black-lookin' rascal, I think ye're nothin' but a gamblin' man! What the major wants with ye, dear knows, but he's yonder in the adjutant's office."

"Couldn't he wait, miss?"

"It's Mrs. I'm Mrs. Ser-rrgeant Malloy. Don't keep the major waitin', him the post commander while the colonel's on sick leave—an' full o' the rank, so he is!"

"Ah, yes." Bishop stored the information, fishing for more. "His many duties must weigh on him. Civil duties, too, I understand, eh?"

"None I know of."

"Well, dear lady, I go my way. If I must, I must, and lonesome with memories to last me many a night. It's my tragedy I found you too late!"

"Argh, for pity's sake go 'long with ye," she said. "I know ye're no good. Go 'long!"

He led his horse back across the parade ground, passing a few troopers who looked at him with only ordinary curiosity. The adjutant's office, a long building of bare planks, was raised off the ground so that it had an equally bare porch. Not wishing to be too far from his horse by turning it over to someone to take care of, he tied its reins to a porch rail, thereby disrupting slightly the dismal pattern of rigid conformity.

Stepping up onto the porch, he shoved open a door and found himself in a long office. Quiet men in uniform, company clerks he supposed, wrote down figures and notations on the long ledgers that the Army favored. They, too, glanced incuriously at him. At this shank of the day some were yawning.

He spoke to a man who wore two stripes and a row of foreign ribbons, barred crosswise in the Prussian fashion. The Army of the West was laced with ex-soldiers from the old countries, proud of their decorations although many had deserted their own service. And the ever-present Irish. And battered adventurers from everywhere.

The corporal marched to a closed door and sprang to heel-clicking attention before tapping on it. It struck Bishop as an overdone bit of military punctilio, but the clerks took no notice. A voice responded, the corporal spoke, received a reply, and beckoned quickly to Bishop. He opened the door, clicking his heels again, ushering Bishop into the Presence.

Bishop walked in, heeled the door shut behind him, and asked Major Jennisk, "What's the reason for having me searched at the gate for my guns?"

XVIII

JENNISK darted his sharp round eyes over Bishop's face. He sat at a desk, no one else in the room. "It's a standing order. This is an Army post—"

"And I'm bringing up around five hundred remounts for the army!"

"Driven by Mexicans! Where's Hump?"

"You won't have to pay him off, that's all I need to say. You only pay me. I hold papers on the horses. Clear title." Bishop noted that Jennisk showed no surprise. He must have been getting reports from the marshals. Jennisk had no knowledge of what had happened to Hump, though, so the stiff-necked old marshal was still somewhere behind.

"That Mexican told me he had three hundred head," Jennisk said. "You turn up with five hundred. How?"

That was another thing he didn't know. "We picked up a second bunch. Made five hundred head in all, but we lost a few, maybe half a dozen. You still buying?"

Jennisk nodded quickly. "I've been worrying over how to fill—" He stopped. "I'll take all that pass requirements."

Bishop helped himself to a cigar from a heavy brass humidor on the desk. A falseness lurked here. The deal didn't rest on solid ground. Like the Sandhole when soaked—treacherous below the deceptively solid-appearing surface.

"Meaning you'll take the lot," he said. "They were bred and picked for Army remounts. And as I've told you, their papers are clean."

Jennisk pursed his small mouth in knowing skepticism. "You do a thorough job! I won't look too hard at the papers. The horses—where are they?"

You know, Bishop thought; you know damned well where

they are. "They're coming up," he answered, "about a mile down the trail." He struck a match and fired the cigar. "Send out a squad of your troopers to bring 'em in."

"Your Mexicans are shy, eh?" Jennisk heaved himself up from his padded armchair, with a flabby man's grunt. "I don't wonder! Er, make yourself comfortable."

"Thanks, I will."

Bishop rested one hip on the edge of the desk. He heard Jennisk snap an order, heard the German corporal's clipped, "Yessir," the smart quick-step, and the bang of a door.

He gazed musingly down at Jennisk's brass humidor, after extracting from it four more cigars. Its hinged lid was heavily embossed with the Stars and Stripes, the Eagle, and the cavalry insignia of crossed sabers. A patriotic cigar box, suited to the outer crust of a sham patrioteer, armchair soldier, grafter. As suited to Jennisk as his spit-and-polish German corporal, his runner, orderly, or whatever he was.

Deep in thought, Bishop strolled out of the office to watch a full troop—Troop C—trot briskly out of the fort, every man in correct dress, straight as a ramrod. He did not marvel at their promptness in carrying out Jennisk's command. They must have been held waiting in readiness. This thing was soaked with deceit.

Jennisk said to him, "The sight of our soldiers will scare the devil out of your Mexicans, I don't doubt!"

"Too much devil in 'em," Bishop murmured.

"Mexicans? Give me the regiment and I'd take Mexico!"

The heroic quality that Jennisk strained for made his piping voice shrill, and Bishop turned away without speaking, a little sickened by the bombastic scorn of a nonfighting braggart.

Troop C brought the horses up to the fort and held them for count into the corrals. A captain acting as inspecting line officer called, when they were all in, "Four hundred and ninety-three, I made it," and looked to Bishop for confirmation. Bishop nodded, trying to foresee when and how he'd get it in the neck. It had to come, he was certain.

The procedure went on without a hitch, hastened by the coming dusk. Jennisk jotted down the figures. Formally, he asked the post veterinary for his judgment on the horses.

"They've been driven hard," was the reply, along with a searching glance at Bishop, "but they look good. We'll know better when they're tested for wind and all."

"If they weren't sound animals in every way," Bishop said, "they wouldn't have got here. They've covered a pretty fair distance. Driven hard, yeah."

He lowered his voice to Jennisk. "Call it four hundred and eighty-five. Take the odd eight head to allow for any possible rejects."

"You don't have any time to spare, is that it, Bishop? I'm wondering what happened down there, to put you in such a great hurry!"

"That's none of your concern," Bishop parried. "You've got the horses I contracted to deliver, and more." He sensed the blow soon coming, the ax in the neck. Jennisk was changing his manner toward him since the arrival of the horse herd—becoming sneeringly superior, smug.

"There are others who're wondering, too!" Jennisk said. "Contract? I didn't make any contract with you."

"An agreement, then. I don't have to remind you what it covered."

"We had a talk, you mean. Nothing in writing, nothing signed, no witnesses. Word of mouth doesn't count."

"With you, no! The word of an officer and—h'm!" Bishop held down his temper. "Do we do business or don't we?"

Jennisk looked down at his paunch and drew it in, aiming at a military posture. "It is irregular to purchase re-mounts before they pass all required tests," he stated, raising his voice. "But if you're pressed for time, perhaps we can stretch a point and come to some sort of arrangement. That is, if the vet approves."

"I'd say it's safe to buy 'em, sir," the veterinary told him. "A first-class lot."

"Very well." Jennisk strutted off, jerking his head for Bishop to follow him. Troop C stiffened to attention, faces impassive, only the eyes registering the subtle disparagement that regulars reserved for civilians and unpopular officers. The captain threw a salute which Jennisk barely acknowledged, and Bishop saw the captain's mouth twitch faintly in the ghost of a spitting motion. Major Jennisk was not the most respected ranking officer that Fort Griffin had ever been blessed with.

At the company offices he parted from Bishop, telling him to go on and wait in his office. Chow call had sounded, the clerks had gone off duty, and the German corporal was reverently tidying Jennisk's desk. The former Imperial Guardsman was one member of the garrison, at least, who worshiped rank no matter what kind of man held it. His china-blue eyes rebuked Bishop for the sacrilege of using the major's ashtray.

Minutes later when Jennisk rejoined Bishop, he said, "I'm having bank drafts made out in the total sum of sixty thousand, six hundred and twenty-five dollars. My signature on them is all that's necessary to make them good as gold, payable at any bank having sufficient funds. They'll be government stamped, but no vouchers attached. That's for my protection. I'll be cashing one of the drafts myself!"

"Nothing on them to show what they're paid for, eh?" Bishop nodded. "Just an entry in your ledgers. Can you get away with it?"

Jennisk drummed his fingertips on his desk, glancing impatiently at the door. "I'm procurement officer, disbursement officer, and in the colonel's absence I rank as the acting commanding officer. I'm answerable to nobody here!" He twisted his mouth. "It's the chance I've always looked for!"

"And you're making the most of it!" Bishop commented. "How about Washington, after the bank drafts are cleared and the government accountants get a look at them?"

"Be a long time moving. You don't know Washington. I can retire, go to a foreign country—"

The bang of an outside door interrupted Jennisk. He leaned forward, stilling his nervous fingertips. A voice said, "This is for Major Jennisk. He's waiting for it."

The German corporal tapped on Jennisk's door, got a quick response, and entered, bearing a folder. He saluted, placed the folder on the desk, back-stepped, saluted again, did his about turn and marched out, closing the door.

From the folder Jennisk took two crisp papers which he scanned with care before dipping a pen in an inkwell. He signed both papers with his name and rank, and held the pen out to Bishop.

"This bank draft is yours." He slid one of them forward. "And this is mine. It's made out to your name, of course, for the sake of the record. You'll have to endorse it for me."

Bishop looked at the figures. A slow jolt ran through him. Here came the edge of the ax. "Wait a minute," he said, having difficulty controlling his tone to an even pitch. "This one—mine—is for five thousand dollars. You've made a mistake. Even at thirty-five dollars a head, the price you agreed to pay me, it'd come to nearly seventeen thousand, wouldn't it?"

"It would—but there's no mistake!" Jennisk's eyes were suddenly ugly. "The horses are here in the corrals, and you can't take them out! I know they're stolen horses, regardless of papers!"

"The fact is, on the strength of those papers I figure to collect better than thirty-five a head."

"The mistake is yours then!" Jennisk slapped the pen down before Bishop. "Endorse this bank draft, or by God you'll get nothing! There are twenty United States marshals and deputies down there in town, aching to take you in on suspicion! Do you guess why they haven't?"

"You?"

"Yes, me! I threatened to send a strong complaint to Washington—to the President himself—if they interfered with the delivery of badly needed remounts for the Army. You got here only by my protection, Bishop—and I can take it away, now that the remounts are delivered!"

"Once I leave this fort," Bishop said, "your protection ends in any case. This"—he tapped the second bank draft —"gives you a cut amounting to better than fifty-five thousand dollars! I sign that over to you? Like hell!"

"You don't have any choice! I can hold up payment until the horses are run through every test in the book!" As he spoke, Jennisk stared up into Bishop's face. "I can stretch it out for a week—giving time for whatever's behind you to catch up with you! I can have you locked in the guardhouse right now, for that matter, on any charge I care to throw at you! My word is law here!"

Bishop gazed at the two bank drafts on the desk. So this was why he had been searched at the gate for his guns. Jennisk's order. Even with the whole garrison at hand, Jennisk would not risk putting the ax to an armed and angry man. This was why the marshals had held off, not realizing that they were aiding and abetting a grafter. Slowly, he picked up the bank draft for five thousand dollars and pocketed it.

"You're sure out to get dirty rich, Jennisk," he said.

"I'm not in this damned Army for glory and retirement on half pay!"

The sunset gun boomed; Fort Griffin still kept up the old custom.

"The gates are closing," Jennisk said. "You can't leave the post without a pass from me. Endorse that bank draft!"

Bishop inked the pen and scrawled his signature. With a flip of his finger he sent the bank draft skimming back across the desk. Jennisk slapped clumsily at it, missed, and it fluttered to the floor. Frowning his annoyance, he shoved his armchair around and bent down for it.

Bishop picked up the patriotic brass humidor. He turned it in his fist, and with one long-reaching strike he imprinted the Star-Spangled Banner on Jennisk's thinning scalp. Jennisk bowed down to the floor and stayed there.

To cover the thump of the fall Bishop moved his feet noisily. He listened for sounds of the German corporal on the other side of the closed door, not sure if that model of military punctiliousness was standing there zealously guarding it. His action, though not unthinkingly impulsive, had been unpremeditated up until the last moment: a watched-for expedient. Moving around the desk, he picked up the bank draft and looked down dispassionately at the ungraceful hulk lying on the floor.

Maybe he had killed Major Jennisk, procurement officer, disbursement officer, acting commanding officer of Fort Griffin. He didn't think he had, but if so the official notice might read, *Died in the line of duty*, or some such unwitting irony. A devoted soldier's epitaph. A fate that Jennisk had never anticipated. And there would come the grim investigation: *What evil hand struck down this gallant officer?*

He straightened his coat and set his hat on firmly, and walked to the door, saying, "Major, it's been a pleasure doing business with you." He half-opened the door. "No, don't bother—I know the way out, thanks. Okay, I'll tell him. G'night!"

He stepped into the outer office and closed Jennisk's door behind him. The corporal, standing three paces away with his back toward the door, about-turned. Under the expressionless blue eyes Bishop folded the bank draft unhurriedly and slipped it into his pocket. "Major says you can dismiss," Bishop told him, and gave him one of Jennisk's cigars.

The corporal hesitated before accepting it. He grunted a word of thanks and waited for Bishop to precede him out of the building. Outside, Bishop said, "G'night, Corporal," while untying the reins of his horse from the porch rail. The corporal nodded, staying to watch him mount.

Bishop walked his horse to the corner of the armory, aware that the corporal was at last satisfied and marching off to his quarters. Getting out of Fort Griffin was his next exigency. The gates were shut; even if he'd had a signed pass from Jennisk, there was Rico waiting down the hill to hold him covered with his heavy Remington .58 rifle.

The thought of Mrs. Sergeant Malloy lay on his mind. Mrs. Malloy and her washing. He rounded the armory and held his horse to its walk across the parade ground back to Soapsuds Row, hoping to find her again, hoping his blarney had not yet drained off that large lady.

Lights were springing up behind the identical windows of the little houses. He rode slowly down the double line, peering in at each window, seeing noncoms and their wives and children eating their supper or ending it. Near the narrow street's end, where he had run into Mrs. Malloy he spotted her. She was clearing table. A burly sergeant sat smoking a blackened pipe, his boots off, his red brown face settled in the phlegmatic reverie of an old soldier taking his ease.

Reining in, Bishop took out a coin and tossed it at the house. It rang on the skimpy bit of front porch, and instantly the sergeant was on his feet, but his wife beat him to the door. She flung it open, and in the fan of light she sent Bishop a discreetly unobtrusive nod of recognition. The sergeant pushed in front of her, brows drawn, hands fisted.

"Sergeant Malloy?" Bishop inquired, and got an affirmative nod. "No wish to disturb you and your lady, but I'm a betting man. I made a bet with Major Jennisk," he lied unashamedly, "that the sound of money, this long from last payday, would bring out the best man in the garrison as fast as an alarm to arms! I let him pick his man, and he told me where to find you."

The sergeant unclenched his fists. "Did he, now?" he said pleasedly. His wife looked more skeptical, but not unpleased.

Bishop drew out two gold double-eagles and clinked them together in his hand. "On a different kind of bet I would appreciate two small favors from you."

"Name 'em!"

"There's a scorched hombre of Mexico waiting by the lone oak below the gates. He's made a bet I can't leave the fort without him seeing me. I propose to slip out the door back here that your lady uses when she hangs up the laundry on the clotheslines outside."

"That's against the rules, to—"

"I know, but it's only to win my bet." Bishop spun the two twenties at the porch. "Would you deliver a message to the hombre?"

The sergeant caught them nimbly. As nimbly, his wife plucked one of them from his palm. "What's the message?"

"Tell him how I got out of the fort. Tell him I'm heading north. My name's Bishop."

Sergeant Malloy looked at his wife. She nodded. "Go on an' slip out the back, Mr. Bishop, sir," he said. "I'll bar the door after ye, nobody the wiser. An' I'll deliver the message to the hombre me-own-self."

"I thank you." It was worth another double-eagle, and Bishop sent it after the others. Mrs. Malloy got that one, too. "I'm riding first to the river, you might mention, because my horse wants watering."

He touched his hat to them and rode on the few steps to the small rear door of the stockade, intended for the exclusive use of the women of Soapsuds Row in drying and sunning their laundry. He let down the bars and passed through. Once outside the fort, he heeled his horse to a run.

As he had told the sergeant he would, he rode straight to the river, to a bend of Clear Fork after it curved north around Hell's Half Acre. There he watered his horse sparingly while leading it downstream under the bank, where he left it rein-tethered to an oak stump. Returning on foot to the bend, he waited in a patch of willows for Don Ricardo to show up. The night was not yet full dark. He had purposely chosen a direct course over soft earth. The Don would have little trouble cutting his sign.

"Come on, Rico!" he murmured.

This was a good time to own a gun, any kind of shooting weapon. He wished that he could have taken the time to ransack Jennisk's office for one. Rico, armed with his pair of well tried six-guns besides that damned rifle, held the hunter's end of the chase. This once, perhaps, he'd be too raging mad for caution.

Bishop searched over the ground for a rock of convenient size and weight for throwing. To try ambushing Rico with a rock, nothing more, made a hopelessly unequal contest but once in a blue moon luck rode a last chip.

"Come on, Rico!"

XIX

A DISTANT MUTTER rose and fell, sending forward the sound-
ings of the folds and dips of the land in fast succession.
It leveled out to a hard hammering on the long slant down
to the river.

Bishop dropped the unlighted cigar he was chewing on.
He mentally marked up a merit to his calculation of what
Rico would do when he got the message from Sergeant
Malloy. No time to dash the two miles back down to the
day's camp and gather his *guerreros* for the pursuit. Every
minute was precious, Bishop on the run and carrying off
the money. Rico was coming along, pushing his horse to its
utmost to gain ground and put his quarry within gunshot range before full darkness fell. He was a light rider,
weighing considerably less than Bishop.

Leaning low to follow the tracks, not slackening pace,
he careened across the skyline like a charging Cheyenne
brave. Bishop got a hopeful vision of him launching himself and his mount headlong into the river, but at the last moment Don Ricardo slung the horse half-around in a sliding,
jolting halt. He jumped off and scrutinized the riverbank.

In the early nightfall he made a lean and febrile figure,
all of his movements rapid, driven by the compulsion to
rush on. Then he jerked upright and for seconds stood
motionless. He was listening for far-off hoofbeats to give
him his direction. The silence was punctuated by the snick

183

of a drawn gun hammer. Hearing no hoofbeats, now he was calling upon his sharp senses for signals, perhaps receiving a faint rumor that the enemy was nearby, lying in wait for him.

Holding his breath, not moving a muscle, Bishop waited for him to come searching into the willows. He held the rock ready. Rico wasn't close enough for him to risk a throw, and he stood on the other side of his horse, to its left, holding its reins. The act of throwing couldn't be made entirely soundless. He'd hear it and duck. A miss, then his advance at the willows, guns flaming.

The seconds passed. Don Ricardo's peering swept a half circle that encompassed the river, thickets on both banks, the willows, rocks. He raised the cocked gun as if to shoot—a test to shake the enemy, flush him out if he lay in hiding. For a few more seconds he kept the position, then swiftly his figure rose and he was in the saddle and riding upstream along the bank.

Bishop watched him vanish, knowing what decision he had reached. Figures I cut north from here, he thought. Figures I must have kept to the river so he can't hear or track me. It's what he'd do, in my boots—chin on his shoulder, *cuidado*. Go on the dodge till he got hold of a gun.

He tramped back to his waiting horse, tightened cinch, mounted, and rode downstream. This time, by night, he'd be more careful to avoid the watchful eyes of the marshals. Have to. No more of Jennisk's so-called protection. At any hour the marshal would have vastly greater reason to take him in, hold him for rigorous investigation. And that stiff-necked old marshal racing up from the Donavon ranch . .

They'd never understand how one thing had led to another, each step justified, the whole thing a perfectly reasonable transaction. Or practically. They lacked the broad view-point of the troubleshooter. Intolerance of lawbreaking narrowed their minds.

The *guerreros*, now, that was still another matter. Rico was out of the way for a while, but not his *guerreros;* they were holding Sera in the camp below Fort Griffin. Have to do something about that.

They had built a fire and posted guards out, and one of them rapped a challenge at Bishop over a leveled carbine. The men at the fire came to their feet, as did Sera and Red.

"Don't shoot, hombre, I'm too discouraged to duck," Bishop said. He rode on by the guard to the fire, where he got off his horse and sat on the ground to tug at his wet boots. "Had to ride that damn river, dodging the marshals, and my feet are cold. Whew, what a bust this is!"

"De Risa?" demanded Arturo Tamargo. "Where is he? Why didn't he come back with you?" He stood menacingly over Bishop. "What went wrong?"

"Everything!" Bishop glowered up at him, at all of them. "De Risa—if only I'd had a gun! *He* went wrong! And you're all wrong if you're looking for him to come here and pay off! I guarantee he won't!"

"What? He is gone?"

The guards ran in, joining the rest, all hurling questions.

"Where?"

"Alive?"

"The money—!"

"Headed north, fast as he can ride!" Bishop rasped at them. "Oh, he's alive, all right! Why d'you think he made sure I didn't have a gun? Tried to kill me after the sale went through. Between him and the marshals, I'm lucky to get here," he said truthfully.

"We are cheated? Us?"

"If you doubt it, just wait for him. You'll be waiting a long time. Or go look for him between here and the fort. As for me, I know the route he took. Give me my guns, *por favor*—that's all I came back for." Bishop refrained from glancing at Sera and Red, ignoring them as of no consequence. "There'll be a shoot-out, I ever catch up with him!" Or, he thought, if Rico ever catches up with me.

"What is his route?" Arturo Tamargo growled. "Tell us!"

Bishop shrugged, somberly eying the veteran *guerrero*. "Go pick up his tracks and find out for yourselves."

"Tell us!"

Carbines tipped at him. Scowling, he said, "From a lone oak below the gates he cut around the fort and struck a bend of Clear Fork north of Hell's Half Acre, near a patch of willows. That's where he wanted to shoot me."

Arturo Tamargo impatiently waved away that superfluous detail. "He crossed the river there?"

"No—kept to the west bank, going north."

The *guerreros* hit into their saddles so fast the horses danced. The bad feeling that smoldered between them and Don Ricardo de Risa—and which Bishop had helped to nurture as a possible investment—had not died out. It served as a fire-starter, and the fire of their rage consumed any doubts of Don Ricardo's perfidy.

"My guns, Tamargo!" Bishop called.

Tamargo, throwing him his guns, snarled, "*You* catch up with him? No—that is for us! *Adios, pistolero!*"

They whirled off.

Red gazed after them, blinking, not quite grasping the fact that he and Sera now meant nothing to the *guerreros*. "Let's get out of here before they come back!"

"They won't," Bishop said. "They'll fasten onto Rico's tracks and stick till they spot him. He's dusting north in a hurry, all right—looking for me. And if he slides out of

186

that jackpot he'll be looking for me all the harder!" He
bit into a cigar and lighted it with an ember from the fire.
"We better mosey, though. There's some trouble in Fort
Griffin that the marshals might connect me with. You're in
bad company."

"Not now," Sera told him quietly. "The bad company's
gone."

He met her eyes and held them with his own. "That
doesn't mean you'd go with me, does it?" he said, making
a statement of it, killing the wish that was in him.

"Only if you forced me to."

"I could do that." And hold onto her, whispered a silent
voice inside him. "But how would I keep you with me
when I'm tending to other matters? In my pocket? Which
reminds me." He dug into his pocket and took out the bank
draft that he had endorsed.

"This is a bank draft for"—he turned it toward the fire-
light—"fifty-five thousand, six hundred and twenty-five dollars. Good as gold, I'm told. It's payment for the horses.
It's yours." He gave it to her.

She accepted it with a quiet, "Thank you," as if expecting nothing less from him, as if her faith in him had
never wavered. He felt grateful to her for that.

Red, staring incredulously, finally exclaimed, "I was dead
wrong, Sera! Bishop, I take back all I've thought and said
against you!"

"Don't strain yourself!" Bishop grunted. "I didn't give
it to you. Sera, you bank it and keep your eye on it. He
might do at horse ranching, but he's a lousy poker player."

He picked up the reins of his horse. The thing was over,
finished; he hadn't quite broken the old code, not yet,
though he guessed he got closer to it with each year of
his life. Like Rico. Like many others, survivors of the wild
fraternity, remnants of the bright flame.

Sera came up behind him and touched his arm. He moved it away. "We're parting company," he said, his back to her. And the silent voice cautioned: Girl, don't make it too hard. I could force you to go with me, and hell take the Texan!

He swung up into his saddle. *Deep seat in the saddle and a faraway look* . . . "I won't be going your way," he said.

They caught each other in Santa Fe, in the gambling room of La Fonda where bright lights glowed and mirrors glittered and a white chip was five dollars.

It was an even catch, a stand-off. From a poker table Bishop saw Don Ricardo enter from the lobby, and Don Ricardo spied him in the same instant and halted stockstill.

The territorial governor of New Mexico was in residence at the old Palace of the Governors, just across the Plaza. Because of the consequent prevalence of heavy law in attendance all about the ancient capitol city, each held fire. Each studied the other for his immediate intentions.

Bishop cashed his chips and got up from the game. Slowly, they came face to face.

"Drink first, Rico?"

Don Ricardo nodded stiffly. He looked hard-used, tired, poor. They paced side by side into the barroom and stood up to the bar, and drank in silence until Don Ricardo muttered, "A hell of a trick!"

Bishop poured another round from the bottle. "Trick? Which one?" The question drew a bitter glance. "Oh—that. Well, you see, I put a dent in the major's skull—he tried to rook me—so what with that and the marshals on tap, it meant a quick vamoose. I left a message for you."

"I got it—and raced north after you! North, the sergeant told me. First to the river to water your horse, then north. I tracked you as far as the river. Where did you go from there?"

THE MUSTANG TRAIL

"I cut back to camp, on—hum—an afterthought," Bishop said. "To see Sera about something. And the Texan."

Don Ricardo sighed faintly. "And to set my *guerreros* out after me! I have been on the run from them ever since! They are positive I double-crossed them. They hunger for the money and thirst for my blood! And here I am dead broke."

"Tough," Bishop commiserated. "That major—Major Jennisk. I heard he struck hardpan too. They found funny doings in his books, and supplies gone missing, including Henry repeaters and all. He stood court-martial. Got kicked out of the Army."

"The money for the horses, where did it go?"

"To Sera, most of it. I held out five thousand, as earned commission—a horse dealer's cut."

"And Sera, where is she?" Don Ricardo asked softly, his dark eyes burning. "With you?"

"No, she went off with the Texan. To raise more horses. And raise kids. Or rob graves and cart bones, for all I know."

"So?" The dark eyes grew reflective. "But I thought you had a strong fancy for her. I was sure of it!"

Bishop shook his head. "No," he lied. "She could do too many things too damned well, for all her small size. Shoot a rifle, handle horses, climb cliffs in the dark, and swim a hellsight better than I can. About all I could beat her at was a fast draw—and when I got to thinking about it I couldn't see that as a fit basis for honeymooning. Anyhow, it was the Texan she wanted. No accounting for taste, eh?"

"I should have shot him!" said Don Ricardo. "And you, too, while the chance was mine! Everywhere I go, the *guerreros* hunt me out. They will not believe that I didn't double-cross them and run off with the money. I am desperate!"

"I've known desperate desperadoes to hide out and lie low till the hunters got tired of looking for him."

"It costs money to hide out. Those devils don't give me time to stop anywhere long enough to raise any! They are worse than your federal lawmen! Worse then the *rurales!*"

"You say you're busted flat, but here you came into La Fonda. This place is expensive."

"I learned you were here."

"H'm!" Bishop paid the bartender. "Well, Rico," he said evenly, "you found me. D'you want us to go off somewhere and swap shots? There's plenty of empty country all round. Rifles or six-guns, take your choice. Guess I owe you the satisfaction."

Don Ricardo gazed at his reflection in a polished back-bar mirror. What he saw brought displeasure to his lined and unshaven face. He turned his back on the bar.

"An hour ago I would have accommodated you. I would have rushed at the chance! Now . . ." He scratched mood-ily at his soiled shirt. "Is it nerves? Is it the drinks? Or is it that I know, behind my rage, that I would have rel-ished playing the same shattering trick on you?"

"You damn near had me!" Bishop said.

"A true enemy is better than a false friend," Don Ricardo went on meditatively, "and the surest way to keep an enemy is to humble him by doing him a condescending favor."

With that bit of philosophizing delivered, he placed his hands on his hips and cocked his head, in parody of his old jauntiness.

"Condescend to loan me the money to go into hiding, and I shall remain your true enemy, ever on the lookout to take my revenge and skin you!"

Bishop grinned at the improbable idea of Don Ricardo de Risa ever being humbled. Still, that was right enough

—a true enemy was better than a false friend. He and Rico had come through a lot together, each recognizing the other's dependable worth, never forgetting the unsettled scores between them. Between old enemies and old friends the line sometimes thinned to a hair, in the pinch.

"All right, I'll stake you to a thousand or two," Bishop said. "Pick your hideout and I'll ride there with you. I'll help you throw the *guerreros* off your trail. Give you a hand if they catch up. That humble you enough?"

"I am humiliated!"

"Good! Come on, let's get going."